Y0-BIX-766

The Day of the Donkey Derby

by the same author

EVERY INCH A LADY
TO MAKE AN UNDERWORLD
HOW TO LIFE DANGEROUSLY
YOU WON'T LET ME FINNISH
ALAS POOR FATHER
GRIM DEATH AND THE BARROW BOYS
YOUNG MAN, I THINK YOU'RE DYING
HELL'S BELLE
KILL OR CURE
NO BONES ABOUT IT
MIDNIGHT HAG
NOTHING IS THE NUMBER WHEN YOU DIE
THE CHILL AND THE KILL
DEATH OF A SARDINE
WHEN I GROW RICH
IN THE RED
THE MAN FROM NOWHERE
MISS BONES
MALICE MATRIMONIAL
MAIDEN'S PRAYER
YOU CAN'T BELIEVE YOUR EYES

The Day of the Donkey Derby

by

Joan Fleming

G. P. PUTNAM'S SONS
NEW YORK

FIRST AMERICAN EDITION 1978
Copyright © 1978 by Joan Fleming
All rights reserved. This book, or parts thereof, may not be reproduced in any form without permission.

SBN: 399-12263-X
Library of Congress Cataloging in Publication Data
Fleming, Joan Margaret.
   The day of the donkey derby.
   I. Title.
PZ3.F62845Day 1978 [PR6011.L46] 823'.9'14 78-9376

PRINTED IN THE UNITED STATES OF AMERICA

The Day of the Donkey Derby

7.00 A.M.

It is nothing unusual for the telephone to ring at seven o'clock in the morning but I was in a particularly delicious sleep, having spent most of the night expediting the birth of the Robinson twins, two fine boys. As I surfaced from the depths I remembered that it was the day of the Donkey Derby and the sun was forcing itself through the gap in the curtains with real enthusiasm. The birds were singing like crazy and the cuckoo was hiccuping that it was time he was on his way: it seemed to be a splendid June day. I must remember, I thought, that I had promised to take some hurdles along to the field we call the playground where the point-to-point course started every spring, to mark off the course for the Donkey Derby. I rolled over and lifted the receiver. 'Dr Lavenham . . .'

'Is that you, Dad?' Much as I dislike being called Dad I answered enthusiastically; it was our son Robin, a doctor and newly qualified surgeon, who was doing a year as surgical registrar at Trinity Hospital, London.

'You're early, Robin!'

'Late, you mean,' he croaked. 'I was just off to bed at five-ten when we got a ruptured ectopic in.'

'God help you, at five ac emma!'

'I think she'll do all right, anyway: Dad –' a slight pause – 'I'm going to be married.'

'Fine, that's just fine, Robin!' I laughed joyfully. 'Which of them is it?'

'Not any of the ones you think; it's a Chinese girl.'

'Fine, fine,' I shouted absently; absently because I was

suddenly acutely self-conscious; this was the kind of moment when fathers show up as the best, or the worst ever. I had to play this perfectly but I wished it was not so early in the morning and that I had had time for a wash and brush up.

'Chinese! That's interesting . . .' Hell! It is so easy to sound like a parody of oneself.

'She's a doctor, doing a pædiatric course here, you know . . .'

'No,' I said vaguely, 'I don't think I . . .'

'Well, Mum will remember; I've often told you about her. Her name is Juniper, Juniper Ah Mee.' Well, thank goodness she's not Wee Tin Po, I thought absurdly.

'What?'

'I didn't say anything, Robin, but I'm thinking: "what a charming name!"'

'She's a charming person, she's got everything, Dad! You're going to love her. Well, listen: I wanted to bring her down to see you but I don't think I've slept for about three days and nights, and Juniper won't wait. She has a couple of days off and she wants to meet you both and she says she'll come alone. That's pretty brave of her, don't you think?'

'We'll be delighted to see her, Robin. It's Saturday, a lovely day by all appearances and I'm taking an afternoon off. It's the Donkey Derby.'

'The what?'

'Oh, never mind. What train will she come on? The two-fifteen . . . she can stay the night, can't she?'

'If that's okay?'

'It's certainly going to be.'

'Good! Thanks! Now I'm going to sleep all day and with a bit of swopping around I may be able to get down tomorrow to bring her back.'

'Fine, Robin, fine. We'll see you then . . .'

It is a mistake, I thought as I carefully replaced the receiver, to call your son Robin; Robins are like Peter Pans, permanently enchanting, giggling boys with locks of hair dropping down over their eyes and unpleasant sniffs which cause you to say all the time: 'Where on earth is your handkerchief, Robin? Well, for heaven's sake get one and use it!' Then suddenly they are stern men, or at least they look it, colleagues with whom you dispassionately discuss an ectopic.

I drew back the curtains and the whole sparkling day enveloped me and because I seemed to stand in a lacuna of sadness I gave a wild laugh and leaped on top of my wife. 'Go away!' She buried her face in the pillows. 'I'm asleep.'

I bit her ear. 'Wake up! It's the day of the Donkey Derby.' No response; I lay still for a moment, then I said very clearly and distinctly: 'Robin is going to be married!' That did it, she was awake instantly, wriggling round to face me. 'Who to?'

'A Chinese girl called Ah Mee – Juniper.'

'Oh God!' I sat up and so did she: we faced one another grimly.

'I think she's doing children,' she said thoughtfully. 'A pædiatrician.'

'Yes, she is.'

Absurdly we each reached for the other's hand. 'This is our moment,' I murmured. 'So far we've never been put to the test.'

'Well, we must kill the fatted calf,' my wife said thoughtfully. 'As I've ordered a leg of pork for the weekend I'd better cancel it.' She reached for the telephone which stood between our two beds.

'The butcher won't be open yet,' I reminded her.

'Of course not!' She sat absently running her fingers gently over her face.

'Why cancel it?'

'She may not eat pork.'

'That's Moslems,' I said, 'or is it? But better not take any risks.'

'We'll literally kill the fatted calf and have a big piece of stuffed veal for dinner; why not? They all eat that, Moslems and Buddhists and Shintoists and Taoists and the lot . . . don't they?'

I nodded and there was another long silence.

'I wonder what Miss Cloverley-ffane is going to think?' my wife said.

It is no good saying I couldn't care less what Miss Cloverley-ffane (with two small f's) thought; she is our mother's help, or rather was, for she has graduated to being our mainstay; without her, our household would collapse because there has always got to be someone at home to answer the telephone when we're out, and apart from her fortnight's holiday, which she takes every year with 'a friend', she serves that splendid purpose. She has some very distinct idiosyncrasies but over the years we have adjusted ourselves to them; we grapple her to our souls with hoops of steel because we would have difficulty in finding anyone as useful.

My wife calls her 'our Mrs Tiggywinkle in a musquash coat' and, indeed, she is a little teapot-shaped object; she can hardly see over the driving wheel of her Mini car. In our time we have been able to treat successfully difficulties in her menopause, several tiresome gumboils and her varicose veins; she is utterly devoted to us. But it was, however, with a small feeling of relief that I remembered it was her day off; uninterested in Donkey Derbys, she had arranged to call for her 'friend' and they were both spending a day on one of the river steamers, her 'friend' providing the lunch. We would be free to feel our way with our prospective daughter-in-law without the Clover's watchful eye upon us. I use inverted commas for Clover's 'friend', neither of us like this tiresome 'friend'.

8.00 A.M.

We have breakfast at eight and patients are expected to telephone between eight and nine, at which time I leave the house for our communal surgery where my partners and I meet for a discussion of the day's work. One of us stays to take surgery and the other two set off on our rounds.

In order to avoid continual jumping up during the bacon-and-egg session, the downstairs telephone is placed upon the table at my right, together with my appointment pad. As I seem so rarely to see my enchanting wife, breakfast is the only time at which we can discuss life, literature, art and the theatre; by evening I am dead tired, sick of other people's troubles and fit only to read the newspaper and the weeklies. For this reason Miss Cloverley-ffane tactfully has breakfast by herself in her room before making the beds.

We live in an old house on the outskirts of the market square of what used to be a sleepy English wool town now far from sleepy; the kitchen is a large one, overlooking the garden at the back and we have our meals in it at a large scrubbed-top table. Thus my wife can fry and boil and roast and serve-up without being out of my sight, which is very pleasant.

'... and their children will have those funny sloping eyes,' she said.

'Nothing funny about them,' I rebuked. 'Oriental; merely epicanthus.'

'... and yellowish flat faces.'

'It is only a matter of getting used to it; they think *we* have fearfully odd faces. Consider what a mixed bag we British are: Angle, Dane, Celt: we've thin pointed faces, flabby fat ones, red, white, yellow, grey. One can't point to one of us and say with any certainty: "There's an Englishman," but you can to a Chinese and say without any doubt: "There's a Chinaman." '

'Not at all! It would probably be a Japanese!'

I laughed immoderately; I remember that laugh well because it was the last I had for quite some time. 'Do you mean to tell me,' I exclaimed, 'that you don't know the difference between a Chinese and a Japanese?' This was rather unfair as I had spent a short uncomfortable time in a Japanese prison camp but the telephone rang and prevented what would no doubt have been a witty reply.

Once as medical students we were discussing whether we would choose a wife who was a good lover or one who was a good cook, when it was my turn to say which I would prefer I said I would seek for neither but one who was witty. As it turned out I got more than my fair share: she is all three.

I picked up the receiver: 'Dr Lavenham . . .' A foreign accent told me he was speaking for Mr Rainbarrow of Dedend House who wished me to come immediately.

'What is the trouble?'

'He wishes you to come at once, it is extremely urgent.'

My partners and I, by mutual agreement, fall over backwards giving absolutely equal treatment to both National Health and private patients. Rainbarrow was a private patient of mine and seemed to enjoy excellent health in that I had only once been of service to him, years ago when he had a prostate gland successfully operated on by a genito-urinary man who had qualified with me at Bart's. All I had done was to diagnose and send him to this chap and after it was all over I got a short note of thanks from the patient enclosing fifty pounds in notes which he said was a gift from him to me and as it happened to arrive at Christmas time I treated it as such. In strict honesty it would be absurd to say that the memory of that gift of cash did not come to me immediately I heard who was calling. And just because of that I hesitated ... hedged ... stammered ... waffled ... was slow and indecisive ... agreed finally to come at once and bolted out of the house because I felt faintly guilty about the alacrity with which I was answering the call; I was not visiting him under the National Health, but as a private patient.

And we were now on the edge of the real summer during which as a nation we amuse ourselves and astonish foreigners with fêtes and processions, and crowning Queens of the May and having Donkey Derbys, and competitions of every conceivable kind.

I had promised to take up to the playground and 'racecourse' behind the cricket pitch a number of hurdles which we stored in our old stable, and this before lunch; these were not being used for jumping over today, but as a fence to keep the racing donkeys on the approved track.

8.25 A.M.

I am fifty-nine; thirty years ago when I came to the town after the war as a fledgling doctor, Rainbarrow had a junk shop in the old meaning of the word. Nowadays junk shops are the most expensive places in town, manned by harpies who batten on the knowledge that apart from selling to the trade, most of their customers haven't the slightest idea of the value of what they are buying (or selling). But in those days it was a real pleasure to junk-shop and I don't mind saying that our house was partly furnished by things we bought from Rainbarrow, the big old kitchen table, for instance, the chopping block, the glass-covered stuffed birds we have in the bathrooms, the cheese dish which is a rough replica of the Albert Hall and lots of other useful objects. Then he moved, to everyone's surprise, into a large, ugly, red-brick house, built at the turn of the century by a successful businessman, on the site of a much older house in a big park which has since been stripped of its wonderful old Windsor-Great-Park-style oaks and turned into useful farmland. It is an awkward house to get at, because the main railway line to London runs through what used to be the park, bisecting the mile-long drive from the main road to the house.

The level crossing, I must grudgingly admit, was well placed in that the line runs along a slight dip in the parkland and only the roofs of the passing trains can be seen from the lodge gates or the house. There is a Victorian bungalow, now derelict, built in railway brick at the level crossing where the old woman lived who used to open and shut the gates for people going to and from the house, until the beginning of the Drive to Make the Railways Pay. When it was announced that this service would be withdrawn Mr Rainbarrow kicked up a great fuss, trying to get the Member to speak up for its retention and writing letters to the local press. However, British Rail had their way but as a concession had a telephone installed in a small wooden box hanging on the fence beside the gate and connecting with a signal box three-quarters of a mile down the line. The diesel engines bring their trains crashing along that stretch of line at an immense speed and there is a notice on both sides of the gate advising road-users to telephone for the safety signal before opening the gates and passing across. British Rail did their best to prevent accidents by illuminating the notice for night motorists but a few months previously there had been a bad accident, not to local people who all knew the rules, but involving two late visitors to the house, whose car had been caught by a goods train as they were half way across; there had been a shocking mess.

Urgent though my visit was, I did not risk passing across without first telephoning and then waiting for the eight-forty, on which my wife frequently goes up to London, to go rocking by. Even seeing it through the eyes of Betjeman, I am unable to look at the house without wincing. It is so pretentious: it tries to be a French château with its long slate mansard roofs, with diamond-shaped patterns in the tiles, but changes its mind lower down when it is strongly influenced by Harrod's and touches of the Prudential building. There are lancet windows and little elaborate railings sitting on top of turrets, like coronets, and a draughty colonnade. And half-way up, over the front entrance, but so high up that it hurts to lean back to look carefully, there is a large carved terracotta panel representing a scene from the past history of the older house; at a quick glance they look like a lot of one-time Rolling Stones and Rockets but one day, if ever I have time (which I won't), I must examine it to see what it really is about.

It once had some self-important name but everybody refers to it as Dead End, spelt Dedend, quite a suitable name since the drive leads only to the house and not beyond it.

8.45 A.M.

Having wasted a few minutes of my packed morning at the level crossing I jumped out of the car and almost ran to the front door and rang the bell. The door did not spring open instantly and I stood reflecting on the nature of my patient's sudden illness.

Mr Rainbarrow was known locally as an 'old character' and which of us among the nations have a better selection of eccentrics than we British? He was a large fat man with a big red face from which his grey crew-cut hair stood up strongly all over his Teutonic head. Having, as he would happily declare, failed many times to pass his driving test, he rode about on a tricycle with a small outboard motor and L plates. He had a big shopping basket on the handlebars and from it would protrude the various food parcels he had collected in the town. He was always cheerful and talkative, mostly on the subject of food, but I had never heard of anyone being invited to the house to a meal, or even to a drinks party. On the whole, one knew very little about him though he would be delightedly pointed out to visitors to the town, puffing away on his tricycle and wearing what Conolly described as a 'piglet' of a tiny Tyrolean hat with a feather in it. It was almost, I reflected as I rang a second time, as though these old oddities were deliberately drawing attention to themselves, clothing themselves in eccentricity to mask a weak character. I have never yet met anyone looking madly eccentric who, on further acquaintance, did not turn out to be disappointingly dull.

I was about to open the front door and shout that I was there when it was opened by a small foreign manservant, presumably the one who had telephoned, still buttoning his white jacket.

He said something like 'comethizwaypliz' and I followed him rapidly up the stairs, my bulging bag in one hand and stethoscope in the other. He stopped, panting, outside a bedroom door: 'She very ill,' he volunteered and I pushed past him and entered the room. He closed the door behind me.

Very ill? She was dead.

A young girl, beautiful of course, because it seems that only beautiful girls get themselves into this sort of trouble, with a mass of black hair, lay on a single bed from which the candlewick bedspread had been removed and was folded on the window seat. She was wearing a thin dressing-gown and a pyjama top. She was lying on what had been a clean draw-sheet, now a little messy.

I suspended all feelings, such as: 'What a damn shame!' or 'So pretty, it might have been the daughter we never had,' or 'Goddam these amateur abortionists!' For about the third time only in my long career as a General Practitioner, I remembered, word for word, the teaching of our professor of forensic medicine: '*The discovery of a body suspected to have died under circumstances requiring explanation is a common test of the doctor's training . . . His first steps in the examination at the scene and his first opinions may make the difference between muddle-headed indecisiveness and a clean, swift and eventually successful prosecution of a criminal investigation. An error of opinion . . . may . . . cause grave distress, even injustice to innocent persons. No doctor can afford to shoulder lightly the responsibilities of his first visit to the scene of suspected crime.*'

I looked her over slowly and carefully. There was no

doubt whatever that she had undergone an attempted abortion and I guess that she had died either from shock or an air embolism; guessed, because it could only be proved during the autopsy. What I had to decide was: was it self-induced? Or was it done by someone else?

I stood pondering the dreary old question: how long ago had she died? And this is one where an ordinary GP is always left in doubt when it is a question of half an hour or so. As a matter of routine I took her temperature and made a note of it but it would have been foolish to decide that she had been alive half an hour ago when I received the telephone call. The temperature of a body varies so very much according to several factors, the temperature of the day for instance, and the room and body idiosyncrasy enters into one's reckonings, too.

All I was sure about was that she hadn't been dead long.

I sniffed around the young girl's bedroom like a bloodhound, hot on the trail. The drawers of the dressing-table and chest were empty and smelled musty. The wardrobe door was partly open and a white raincoat hung on a hanger, also a blue linen summer suit. A small suitcase, half packed; an open dressing-case, high-heeled sandals. There was a little white linen hat lying among the make-up things on the dressing-table and a pair of black slacks, panties, bra and polo-necked white sweater lay on a chair where she had apparently tossed them when she undressed. The pyjama trousers, too, lay in a tiny crumpled heap, and a silk wrapper. I stared hard at the things on the dressing-table, as though they could tell me something. In fact, they did. Among them lay a ring, a big square amethyst suitable for a slim white hand, worth about thirty pounds. I looked at the left hand of the dead girl: she wore no wedding ring.

There was a handbag, too, which I surprised myself by looking inside. What it contained of interest was a passport in the name of Molly O'Dare, born in the Republic of Ireland, age 22, now living in Chelsea, London, *and* an air ticket to Gibraltar for a night flight, or rather early morning of this very night (very in this case an adjective meaning the night to come of the day upon which I stood staring down at the ticket).

So she had been intending to fly to Gibraltar tonight, had she?

I stared down at her; *shock* covers a number of physical conditions and in this case I guessed death might be sudden collapse from reflex vagal inhibition and if this was so there must have been a second person involved. Women sometimes die of instrumental interference carried out by themselves but there is always a great deal more evidence of injury, and in any case it was unlikely that a young girl of her appearance would carry out the self-mutilation that an older woman might inflict upon herself.

'Dear heart!' I heard myself exclaim. 'Who did it?'

If she had done it herself the instrument would have fallen from her hand as she died and if so, where was it? This was a perfect example of *muddle-headed indecisiveness* on my part, of which we medical students had been warned. The windows were shut, the room was desperately hot and stuffy, the sun had been shining in and was now moving away. I thrust my stethoscope into my bag, giving myself time to think, and slowly left the room.

As I walked down the wide shallow staircase, it creaked loudly, and I descended into the great pitchpine panelled hall which was more like a Unitarian Chapel of the mid-nineteenth century than the hall of a house where people actually lived.

From one of the doors which had been standing open Mr Rainbarrow came out smiling. He was always smiling and it was not long before I realized that his was not a cheerful face, as I had always thought, but a big red face with a rictus, a flower with a two-lipped corolla, or a great unhealed gash. I felt an immediate revulsion as from the sight of something loathsome. I think my mouth went dry and I said nothing but stared at him. I don't know what expression was on my face but he came towards me in a friendly manner and said urgently: 'How *is* the poor girl?'

9.25 A.M.

I walked across to the hall table which was like an offertory table, put down my bag and when I turned round Rainbarrow had been joined by the manservant and a woman. Hideously inappropriate replies on the lines of: 'No better than when you last saw her, I am afraid,' crossed my temporarily disordered mind but I managed to keep them behind the barrier of my teeth. I said nothing. I stood by the table till my saying nothing amounted to high drama and the couple ran upstairs, along the landing and apparently into the bedroom while I stood and stared at Rainbarrow and he stood smiling in my direction. After about twenty-five seconds I heard the sounds of amazement and distress which I had half expected and the couple came down and surrounded Rainbarrow with cries and lamentations in broken English and Spanish. Rainbarrow, still smiling but now frowning at the same time, hurried up the stairs, followed by the servants. He too was back within the minute: 'This is a dreadful thing, Doctor, truly dreadful. What happened?'

I cleared my throat and found to my surprise that my voice would work. 'That is exactly what I would like to know, Mr Rainbarrow,' I said, and quite pleasantly too.

'I shall tell you, my dear fellow. This poor young guest of mine came downstairs early this morning, fully dressed, to make herself a drink. I found her in the dining-room, at the sideboard, looking for the gin, she said. She had a very bad pain. She was crying. I gave her a gin, together with two aspirins, and helped her back to bed. A little later I sent Encarnita here up to her room and she found her in a state of collapse.'

That, roughly, was what he said, together with a great deal more on the same lines which is not worth recording. I don't know exactly at what moment there appeared hostility between us because I deliberately said more or less nothing, I grunted and clicked my tongue and nodded my head and uttered no two coherent words but somehow or other the situation began to harden *against* me. Finally I asked where the telephone was because I wished to use it. He asked me bluntly why I wished to use it and I said, looking at my watch, that it was now half past nine and if I wanted to get in touch with the Coroner about an inquest before he left his home for the Court, I should do so immediately because I had a busy day in front of me.

'But, Doctor . . .' and there was the usual spate of protest; I could not understand why the Spanish couple stayed with us all the time, close together and staring.

'Who is this young girl?' I interrupted at last. 'Who on earth is she?'

Rainbarrow was a bit fussed now, I could see. She was a niece of his, he said, just a niece and I could see by the way he moved his hands, if by nothing else, that he was lying. It was now his turn to ask a direct question. 'What did she die of, Doctor?'

'Shock,' I said, 'probably, or maybe an air embolism following an attempted abortion. Or perhaps vagal inhibition.'

'Vagal what?'

The sudden silence and cessation of fidgeting made me pause in my prowl round the hall looking for the telephone. 'It was either self-attempted or . . . someone else did it. As the circumstances of her death require an explanation, I have no other alternative but to telephone to the Coroner. You must understand that,' I said, looking from one to the other of my audience of three.

'But surely . . .'

'Yes, Mr Rainbarrow?'

'Surely . . . ?'

'It is impossible for me to sign a death certificate,' I pointed out, reasonably enough. 'I am satisfied that there was an attempted abortion and only an autopsy will show exactly how she died. But it was sudden, almost immediate.'

'Oh, poor young girl,' he cried and a lot more of that sort of thing. I was beginning to feel extremely sick; the squeamishness which I had to try hard to overcome when I first took to medicine seemed to be coming up at me again.

I shouted: 'Where is that damn telephone?'

'. . . why did she do such a thing? . . . What possessed her?'

'The telephone!' I cried, with no hope of anyone hearing me or taking any notice if they did.

Then I noticed that I had become part of a conspiracy; the three were standing in a closed-in group round me and Rainbarrow was saying things which so astonished me and caused me to think so rapidly that I could hardly keep my mind on what he was saying, which amounted to the suggestion that I should sign the death certificate now and that would be that. Family disgrace would be thus avoided and, well, he didn't quite say a good time would be had by all, but that was the basic idea.

'I can't do that,' I said deliberately mildly, rather than stand upon my Hippocratic oath and stoutly declaim things about Honour and Duty. 'For one thing the undertakers will wonder. They can report anything they think suspicious to the Coroner.'

But a sort of pleading for mercy went on and I said much more definitely: 'It is completely impossible for me to sign the certificate or do anything other than get in touch with the Coroner. Apart from every other consideration, there is no instrument to be found. If she used an instrument upon herself it would be found near the body, since she seems to have died instantaneously. She wouldn't have had time to hide it, it would have fallen from her hand.'

And now, looking back and trusting only my visual memory, I knew that for a short time between then and a little later on the only female there was not present. And it is hardly surprising that I failed to notice that she was not there because just about now Rainbarrow, apparently labouring under an even more severe shock than previously, appeared to be accusing *me* of using an instrument.

And the awful thing was that *he could have been right*.

I saw exactly the trap in which I had let myself be caught. I had gone straight upstairs and into the girl's bedroom without any other person with me. I had spent anything from ten minutes to perhaps twenty alone in the room, and had come out, closing the door behind me. There weren't any valid excuses; I deserved everything that was probably coming to me. I'm not one to suffer fools gladly either.

'. . . and you must have the instrument in your bag, Doctor.'

I nodded in accord with myself about fools, but he took it that I was agreeing with him.

'You have?'

I was longing for a moment's respite to think. The machinery I needed for the use of cunning seemed temporarily out of use, jammed. I thought: God! I've got myself into a bloody awful mess now; the fact that one has never had any occasion to be on one's guard is no possible excuse for being off it.

9.50 A.M.

After what might have been a couple of hours but was probably less than a minute, I asked Rainbarrow if we might be alone together and, with a word or two of Spanish, he dismissed the couple.

'Now,' I said, and opening my bag I spread out on the dreadful toffee-coloured table everything it contained which, with the exception of a couple of scalpels for lancing, scissors, ear syringe and diagnostic set, was purely medicinal; my obstetric bag was outside in my Mini.

'There! And if you think there is anything in that lot for procuring an abortion, you have a better imagination than I.' (A doctor's remark in poor taste.) I looked hard at the man and wished I knew more about him; what kind of person was he? I didn't seem to be able to get anywhere near him mentally; he was a kind of stock repertory figure playing a part rather badly. He beckoned me to come into his study but I slowly put everything back into my bag before following him.

He stood beside his desk, admonishing me with a raised finger.

'You're a kind man, I felt that from the time I first met you, and you were most considerate when I had my little trouble some years ago. I'm quite sure you didn't do this thing for gain but out of kindness. I really believe that. A kindhearted man, you would not be able to resist the pleadings of poor Molly. I know only too well how you felt. She comes of very good old Irish family . . . she would have been scared out of her wits at the idea of having a child with no father. If she had asked my advice, I should have told her to go home and make a clean breast of it . . .'

He was talking in ready-made sentences, like a radio play.

'Don't look at me like that!' he snapped. 'All I am trying to say is that I understand.'

'Understand what?'

'How you came to do it. And I don't blame you, I'm only sorry for you. I want to co-operate.'

'You do?'

'Now, now! Don't think I can't hear the edge in your voice. I just want you to know that I shall do my very best for you, and, indeed, for her, for I am as anxious as I can be that her name should not be dragged into the courts over this. It would be terrible for her family, I mean, for the rest of her family,' he added hurriedly after his small slip. 'As I see it, it is perfectly simple: all you have to do is sign the death certificate and we'll get her boxed up and I . . . yes, I'll take her body home to Ireland and try to explain to them . . .'

'Don't be ridiculous,' I shouted. 'She's got to have died of something. Two doctors would have to sign the certificate and at least one of them would have to state that she had been attending him, or he her, for illness of some kind.'

'Now, now! I'm quite sure these things can be avoided; there must be any number of unfortunate young women who die as a result of this kind of thing; what is the use of bringing it all out into the open? It only harms the dead and hurts the living!' His voice became higher and a little shrill. 'It's selfish and pompous to climb on your high horse, to mention your honour as a doctor. What about a little grain of human kindness and understanding?

Eh? What have you got to say about that? What about Our Lord and the woman taken in adultery? Eh? You're supposed to be a good Christian gentleman: what about that? Say something!'

'I'm thinking.' And I was. There was something to think about in what he was saying. I sat down in a chair beside his desk. 'Very well,' I said after a few moments, 'I'll tell you why I am hostile to you. It's because I believe this girl was dead when your man telephoned to me. I think you have tried to trap me. I think there is a lot more behind all this than there appears to be. Why was this girl here? Why did she have to get rid of the baby? If you are the fond uncle you profess to be, why could you not keep her here, away from her family, and let her have the baby here when it was due? And above everything I am against the whole process of abortion. I believe in the girl having the baby, every time . . . it always turns out a good thing in the end. It is never as bad when the baby is actually there and many's the time it has ended in adoration of the little thing by everyone concerned. Often the parents of the girl adopt the baby as their own and the mother of the girl proudly wheels it about, showing it to everybody; the neighbours crowd around, knowing perfectly well whose baby it is, loudly praising it; it happens very often like that.'

He gave a great impatient sigh. 'Well, let me assure you it's not like that in this case. She *had* to get rid of it. There were no two ways about it.'

'Why?'

10.10 A.M.

'Look, Doctor, you've been here well above an hour; you say you've got a busy day ahead of you. Well, so have I. I've got a busy day too, my only busy day in the year, my day of days.' There was a slightly hysterical note in his voice. 'A day upon which I can't afford to have a thing like this happen. It is the only day in the year when I simply do not feel able to cope with it, or with trying to talk you into a reasonable frame of mind. I've got other things to think about, man!' He walked nervously between his desk and the window as he spoke.

'Let's stop arguing, then,' I suggested briskly and turned to go. 'I will get on with my work.'

He stood with his desk between us; he was still wearing that smile but it was now the face anyone would make when something hurts, a wince, permanently in position.

'You're going to the Coroner,' he declared.

'You've got a dead body here,' I pointed out. It would have been too easy to lose my temper and I was near it but in the event it is always simpler not to have done so. If you keep your temper, you have the advantage every time. 'Something has to be done about it. Leaving the Coroner aside for the moment, the undertakers have to be informed, someone has to come to lay out the body, and nobody can do anything constructive till there's a death certificate to say she's died of something. I can't write on it only that she's died of shock or an air embolism, which is what I suspect . . . there's got to be some reason for her shock or embolism. And if I write "due to attempted abortion" there *has* to be an enquiry.'

For a long time he stood thoughtfully tapping his fingers on the edge of the table, murmuring once or twice: 'A dead body . . . a dead body.'

'Come on,' I said irritably, 'I can't stand here arguing all day. *You* telephone to the Coroner; tell him you've got a dead body here and that you suspect I killed the girl, a girl I have never seen in my life before, within the last hour. Go on! We'll see what he makes of it.'

I pulled my small diary from my pocket and told him the Coroner's name and address which I had on the list of telephone numbers at the beginning. 'And I'd hurry if I were you; that body is cooling off quickly; the police surgeon might be able to pinpoint the time of death better than I. I should get on with it,' and I started to leave the room. I heard the sound of a drawer opening and had the weirdest feeling that I would feel the agonizing pain of a bullet between my shoulder-blades when he lumbered heavily in front of me and stood between me and the door actually holding a pistol.

It was an error in tactics of the worst possible kind; it showed me that he was a frightened man and that the situation was so out of control that he had to resort to a desperate, stupid remedy. I despised him.

'I am an old man,' he croaked, pointing the pistol at my midriff with a dead steady hand. 'Seventy!'

'Really? You don't look a day over sixty-nine and you're old enough to know better. Old men shouldn't threaten people with guns; it shows they're nuts.'

'I'm as sane as anyone, I simply don't mean to let you go out of this house.'

'Till when?'

'Till when I'm ready for you to go.'

I thought hard; had I or had I not said anything at

home about where I was going? The last thing I remembered about this morning's breakfast was my boisterous laughter at my own joke. There is no kissing of the wife goodbye, such as I believe businessmen indulge in, in our house. I very often bang down the receiver and tear out without a word to anyone; I may be back in ten minutes and have an extra cup of coffee, or I may not return till three o'clock when my lunch is congealed to a solid mass in the bottom oven of the Aga cooker, with an enamel plate over it. I *might* have expressed surprise, I might have said, 'Mr Rainbarrow in trouble,' as I put down the receiver but it was unlikely because this morning both my wife and I had our minds full of our early news from our son Robin.

He was almost hopping about with impatience. 'I'm not having you going to the Coroner with your story, no sir! He's having *my* story first. I'm not letting you loose to go and do it again, not me!'

I said: 'You know that by detaining me you're invalidating anything you may have to tell . . .'

'I can't argue with you any longer,' he interrupted and then something made me slew round towards the window where my little car should have been standing, immediately outside . . . but wasn't.

'Yes,' he agreed, following my glance, 'your car is being taken care of, in one of the stables.'

'I merely wondered if one of my partners was here yet,' I said casually. 'We're going on a case together this morning and I told him to call here for me if I was delayed because he does not know where we are going.' It was a hasty and unsuccessful fib.

'If he calls he will be told you left some time ago,' Rainbarrow said through his ghastly smile, 'but if he agreed to meet you here, I cannot imagine why you are in such a hurry to get away. I'd rather you didn't leave till I'm ready. Will you kindly lead the way across the hall. I promise you that if you make any move to escape I shall put a bullet through your leg. I am an excellent shot and I don't want to hurt you more than I need; one dead body at a time is quite enough . . .'

We walked across the hall, through the green baize doors which swing open both ways and along the passage of what used to be called 'the servants' quarters' to the pantry.

'This is one of the reasons why I bought this house,' he said, opening the door of the silver safe. 'I used to get the willies about being accidentally locked up in here so I took steps to make it reasonably comfortable.' Still holding the pistol, he turned on a switch with his other hand, which started up two electric fans, one for the intake and the other for the extraction of air. 'It's fresh enough, they each lead along an air tunnel to the outside wall in a similar way to those marvellous grates.' The silver lay, tied up in old-fashioned green baize bags, in weird shapeless chamois bundles and in leather-covered cases along the shelves.

I turned and faced him: 'I'm not going in there, you know!'

'Just for a short while,' he returned comfortably, 'until you have had time to make up your mind about signing that death certificate.'

'I've made it up,' I answered grimly.

'You have? Well done, sir, well done!'

'But, as I told you, it will have to be signed by two doctors.'

'One of your partners . . . excellent!'

'*Not* one of my partners. A young doctor whose train from London I am meeting after lunch. I will bring the young doctor here with me and together we will examine the body, and we shall see . . .'

'I don't want any half promises.'

Meantime I was measuring the distance between us and trying to remember from the films I had seen exactly how James Bond had managed to un-arm practically anyone who drew a revolver on him. I'm fairly active for my age but unfortunately out of condition; the only thing I could think of was a well-aimed kick but he must have known all about that because he was standing at least six feet away and holding the gun steadily.

'It's not a half promise,' I said, 'and I must remind you that if you locked me up in here, you'd be absolutely damning yourself. No one is going to believe I invented the story; I'm not known locally as a nut; on the whole I've been thirty fairly crime-free years in my practice and there isn't any reason why I shouldn't be telling the truth when I try to get you certified.'

'I've had no reason to do anything but respect you, Doctor, till you come rushing into my house, on a call from my manservant and performed such a hurried illegal operation on a girl that she expired.'

'It is so absurd a story that no one would believe you.'

'It won't sound quite so absurd when a bundle of split new five-pound notes is found in your bag to the tune of five hundred pounds.'

I'd left my bag on the hall table.

10.40 A.M.

And incidentally all that talk about getting him certified was a lot of nonsense; since the Mental Health Act of '59, you can't get anyone certified until they're actually foaming at the mouth and roaring around with carving knives; even then there have to be twenty-eight days at the recommendation of two doctors whilst Mental Welfare Officers make up their minds. There's no such thing as 'lunatics' and 'imbeciles' now, we're all 'subnormal', 'severely subnormal' or 'psychopaths' and if we're really murderously inclined it is: 'Seriously irresponsible conduct on the part of the patient.'

So if I were to present myself at the office of whatever authority I chose and tell them that I had been called to the house of an old patient, had found the newly dead body of a young girl, had been accused of procuring an illegal abortion and, on denying it, had been led at the point of a gun to a plate safe into which I was locked until such time as he was inclined to let me out, he would probably listen with interest and the answer would be: 'So what?'

'What are you smiling at, Doctor?'

'Was I smiling? Merely a nervous twitch, I assure you; but anyway, I've got something to smile about, haven't I? Five hundred pounds in the bag, did you say? I can hardly believe it. I get all sorts of presents from various grateful patients, such as for instance a Muslim rosary, a tinned Chinese duck and a translation of Horace's Odes done by the chap who presented me with it; five hundred pounds in notes as a gift! You have unrealistic feelings with regard to the Income Tax Inspector's clutching hand, I must say.'

'Stop talking and get inside.'

I ceased to feel flippant and whimsical and in a mood for wise-cracking. All these years, day in and come another day, I'd spent my mornings, my afternoons and most of my evenings attending to coronary thrombosis, bronchitis, varicose ulcers, hæmorrhoids, tonsils ... I had become an automaton like the wretchedly tired doctor who, when being shown an intimate part of the body late at night, inadvertently murmured: 'Say ah!'

Here I was, well over the edge of *something different*, something *new*, and I was playing at it.

'Right, you and I had better come to terms, Mr Rainbarrow. If you really have got that amount of money to throw about, there may be a situation here worth discussing. There's nothing you can't do with money,' I heard myself declaring; 'Money talks! I admit I was bluffing when I said one of my partners would call for me here; he won't. Nobody knows where I am and they won't start worrying till lunch-time. I'll get that death certificate signed for you. I'll just have to think out what we're going to put on it and I'll get this doctor friend I'm meeting shortly and we'll put our heads together over it. No need to worry any more on that score.'

I was going to ask brightly if there was anything else I could do for him but realized from the look on his face that I might easily go too far.

He frowned with his mouth still stretched. 'I can't believe you've changed your mind over a few pound notes. It's impossible!'

' "There's no use trying, one *can't* believe impossible things," ' I said, watching to see if he recognized the quotation from *Alice* and when he didn't, I quoted the Red Queen's reply: ' "I dare say you haven't had much practice," ' to see what he would say, but he said nothing and breathed heavily. He had the blown-out look of people who over-eat grossly. I wondered if he had extremely high blood pressure; but that would be too easy a way out.

'I'd like to take your blood pressure,' I murmured. 'Isn't all this a bit too much for you, Mr Rainbarrow?'

I think I had touched him in a sensitive spot but I was not sure; his hand did not falter as he held the gun towards me.

'For instance, there is not the slightest need to hold that heavy pistol. I assure you it is unnecessary; I'm on your side. I won't go, I promise. I want that five hundred pounds too much; it would make all the difference to me, you know. So I'm with you from now on, not against you.'

11.00 A.M.

Soon I was sitting on a velvet-covered Knowle settee in the large gloomy drawing-room and he, still breathing abnormally heavily, was setting out exquisite cut glass tumblers and a bottle of that splendid Highland whisky which is bottled in its natural state, almost colourless. I could do with any amount of it. Like Tweedledum, I thought: *I'm very brave generally but today I happen to have a headache.*

'I always have mine with Malvern water,' he said, handing me half a tumbler of the stuff.

'I don't,' I said, draining the water into a saucer containing a plant. He poured out a half-tumbler for himself and filled it up with mineral water.

I sat back and relaxed while the whisky behaved in my stomach like a lighted Catherine wheel; it wouldn't do my gastric ulcer any good but it was doing wonders for my morale.

I stared at the fireplace in amazement; on either side there was a foot-high carved figure, each behaving oddly; the woman had torn down the front of her marble frock, leaving one breast exposed and was pointing indignantly at the carpet, or else the damage had been done by the man on the opposite side who, half naked, was apparently doing the first few steps of the hornpipe with a small scroll in his hand, raised above his head, which was turned towards the woman and he was wearing a lecherous leer on his face. All in rather dirty white marble. A cross little electric fire stood between them; my host had quite unnecessarily lighted one bar for my comfort on this hot summer day.

It was a large room, comfortable and furnished with considerable opulence, if not good taste; everything was bulbous, like the owner himself, and highly ornate. There were a couple of what I took to be extremely valuable commodes and a tallboy in Queen Anne chinoiserie, the base of which was a tangle of *Fantastick* legs, all gilded and drawing attention to themselves. And there was a marble-topped table with a base so rococo that the *Roi Soleil* himself would have approved of it; it was probably French and a museum piece.

I turned my attention to Rainbarrow. He was sitting opposite to me in a wing chair, the gun tucked beside him, his knees apart and his hands hanging loosely between them holding the now almost empty whisky glass; it was an attitude of relaxation because it gave plenty of room for the grand Pickwickian curve of his lower stomach. I looked at his face but he wasn't looking at me; his gaze was wandering absently about the room; he was thinking about something else.

I was worried about having left my bag on the hall table; if he could put a bundle of sterling in it, he could equally well have put the missing instrument in it too; I should have remembered a thing like that.

'I ought to start preparing lunch,' he said heavily, 'I can't get through a day like this without a proper meal.'

'What about your servants?'

He snorted. 'They're Spanish; they can't cook. They keep the house in good condition though; there's a lot of cleaning and polishing to be done and it's too far for any of the local women to come on their bicycles across the park; at least, it shouldn't be but it is.' The alcohol was now coursing pleasantly round my body and must have been doing the same round his; it was the time for confidences but he still did not have his mind on me. He was talking almost to himself.

'That's the worst of women; they are far more nuisance than they are worth. Fancy that girl going and dying on us on a day like this!' He raised his heavy eyes to me: 'That's what I mean about women.'

I nodded sympathetically.

'For the few minutes of pleasure you get out of them, they're just not worth it. People call them the stronger sex!' He blew out his cheeks. 'We should never have had universal franchise, I opposed it at the time, I was only a stripling but I was pretty noisily anti the Suffragette movement; one of my aunties was one.'

I nodded again as though in complete agreement.

'Women aren't to be relied on, that's what I've said all along and, by God, I've been proved to be right today, all right.' He blew out his cheeks again. 'Today has been truly bitched-up, that's it! Bitched-up! Those two women . . . Molly is – was – a well-brought-up young lady, educated in Ascot and at a convent school in Spain, she could speak Spanish like a native. You should have heard her chattering away with Encarnita . . . Her father is a rich landlord, one of those whose grandfather starved peasants to death . . .'

He looked up and stared across at me, seeing me now, but I looked away. It was all perfectly simple to me now and I didn't want him to know that I had seen the light. Molly, whoever she might be, had become pregnant and had recently talked it over with the Spanish woman who had offered to put things right for her perhaps early this morning. And early this morning, shortly before my telephone call . . . the Spanish woman had botched it. And the male, husband of Encarnita, or boy-friend or whatever, had been called upon to get a doctor as soon as possible.

Basically simple but complicated by something bigger behind it all.

'How long have you had Encarnita?' I asked casually, holding up my whisky glass and studying it at eye level.

'They've been with me about eighteen months. They never stay with me long, these Spanish couples; they hurry back home to their lousy country with the money they've made. They don't really like it here. They send other couples they know to take their places; it works fairly okay except that you get sick of the constant change. And they can hardly ever speak English; they may understand a little but most of them can't wrap their tongues round English; they won't even try. Or when they do make an attempt, you can't make out what they're trying to say. This youth isn't bad, though.' He looked at his wristwatch for what was, I reckoned, about the fifteenth time in the past hour.

So it was certainly not the Spanish couple he had been trying to protect and I didn't think, either, that he had been driven by any affection for Molly. I didn't think that the girl's death had affected him emotionally at all: he had put on a fairly poor show of being upset about it. He was more like a man who has missed a train for an important interview; exasperation, irritation and even desperation had motivated him since I had come into the house. Never affection, fondness or goodwill.

He leaned back in his chair and breath-whistled a tune from *The Mikado*: 'a wandering minstrel I, a thing of shreds and patches . . .' His foot tapped in time to the tune.

'What time is this doctor friend of yours arriving, eh?'

I told him. He resumed his whistling: '. . . of ballads,

songs and snatches . . .'

'You'll be with us for lunch then . . .' It wasn't so much a question as a statement; he knew damn well I would be there for lunch because he wasn't going to let me go.

I shrugged my shoulders and didn't say so, but yes, I would be with them for lunch, for tea and dinner too if I hadn't got to the truth. I would be with them for lunch, yes, but I wasn't going to eat a mouthful until I had tried it on the dog first, or rather, until I had seen others eating it. I had entered into the spirit of the thing; I'd been threatened with a gun, accused of committing a crime and bribed with five hundred pounds in the last hour; I was getting the hang of it now. It dates me badly to be able to remember Gerald du Maurier as Bulldog Drummond but I think that I have carried that image in my subconscious since I was taken to see the play at Wyndham's Theatre as a schoolboy. For suavity, sang-froid and general smoothness of manner overlying a mind as alert as a ferret, it would be impossible to find his equal. I now crossed my feet and put them up on a nearby footstool, I again raised my whisky glass and this time looked at it with one eye screwed up.

'I shall be here for lunch, yes,' I said languidly. 'What are we going to have?'

11.20 A.M.

The pistol lay there cosily beside him and I felt as uncomfortable and self-conscious about it as though my Labrador had misbehaved himself on the carpet (not that he ever would). I couldn't, as it were, be natural in its presence. My discomfort was increased because when I had put down my empty glass I had nothing to do with my hands. I don't smoke because I always have something in my hands and a cigarette would be a nuisance; if it is not a pen, at the ready to sign a form which I do on an average once every ten minutes in the ten working hours, it's a thermometer or my stethoscope. It is so easy for a doctor to take to excessive antidotes, getting out from under the leaden weight of other people's troubles. Very fortunately I have a wife who stimulates my mind to thoughts about other things and a dog who has to have a brisk walk every evening on the hills above our town whatever the weather. So, as I said, I don't smoke and occasionally I feel my hands are in the way. I folded them and sat back but the Knowle settee had too wide a seat and even somebody of my height might feel his legs were dangling. Mine weren't, but I lay back far too far, so that I was neither lying nor sitting. I jumped up and went to one of the windows; it was still a glorious day, though none of the sunshine came into the drawing-room.

'Lovely outlook,' I murmured and there was a rumbling of a passing train and I could see the roofs of the carriages skimming past in the distance and heard the

Continental hoot of the diesel as it approached the level crossing.

Then my thoughts took a turn which caused me to feel a start of excitement.

I turned and looked at Rainbarrow; he was sitting exactly as before, staring down at the carpet.

'Would you like me to take your blood pressure?' I suggested.

He raised his eyes slowly to mine: 'Is the thing for doing it among your traps?'

I nodded. 'I'll get it.'

'No,' he said, struggling up, 'I'll get it.' He picked up the pistol and turned the safety-catch either on or off; as I don't know my way around pistols I could only hope it was off. It was far too big to go comfortably in his pocket but he slipped it inside, with the handle clumsily lolling out, so the catch must have been turned on; otherwise, if the thing had accidentally fired, it would have shot off his right foot.

He brought my bag back, demonstrating to me the bundle of fivers which I took from him and put in the inside pocket of my jacket.

'Now lie down . . .' He took off his jacket.

It was high but not startlingly so. I felt strongly tempted to dramatize the situation, staggering back and exclaiming: '*Good God, man! I give you another half hour at most!*' But habit and the boring old bedside manner were too deeply ingrained. I looked cryptic; that was exactly it, a masterpiece of the cryptic.

Always after taking a blood pressure I have the searching eyes of the recumbent patient on my face and always I hope I look deadpan. I go back to my desk and make notes on the patient's card, still with an expressionless face so that if it is abnormally high, they are not alarmed by my expression and if it is normal they are not disappointed that they are, after all, not ill. Not having a card to write on, I brought out my travelling appointment book and wrote the result any old where. He continued to lie on his back and stare up at the ceiling; I knew he cared a lot what the result was but he wasn't going to let me see he did. I sat on the edge of the wing chair he had vacated.

For a long time I looked at him in silence, then I said gently: 'There is something extra worrying you, isn't there?'

He grunted and blustered and struggled round into the sitting position and even then he couldn't resist a glance at his wristwatch. I wondered if he were really looking at it for any reason or whether it was the compulsive behaviour of a lunatic, who is always looking at the time.

But it wasn't any good; I just wasn't on the beam.

I lightened my mood: 'But you're not feeling up to the mark, are you? You couldn't be, with a blood pressure like that.'

He looked very gloomy indeed.

'Dieting would help,' I murmured. 'You eat too much and you don't get enough exercise.'

'Exercise! You try going to the shops and back on my three-wheeler!' he snorted, but he was paying attention to me now, I could tell.

'You could do without this lunch you are talking of cooking.'

'No, Doctor, you're wrong there. I get ravenously hungry; I can't carry on without food.'

'Certainly not, but you've got a pretty good hump to live on, and you can reduce the amount you eat. One meal a day is quite enough; for the rest, one of the hard-breads spread with Marmite!'

'I'd rather die!' he exclaimed.

'That's not true.'

'Eating is my greatest pleasure, that and enjoying the luxury of my house. Why bother to make money if you're going to live on a bit of hard-bread?' And so on, while I folded my sphygmomanometer and put it away in my bag.

'I'm not having a heavy lunch as meals go. A *blanquette de veau* with creamed potatoes followed by a little Stilton with Bath Olivers . . .' His eye had the greedy gleam in it that my Labrador's has when his meat is being cut up. 'You can come into my kitchen now and watch me slice the veal,' he said magnanimously, 'it has to stew gently for a time before I make the lemon sauce.'

'Ah! The sauce . . .' I said, 'Now that you could do without.'

'Nonsense, the sauce *is* the dish, it's only the stock, lemon juice, butter, the yolk of two eggs and the cream.'

I laughed a little, not that it was a laughing matter. 'Ever heard the old saw about digging your grave with your own teeth?' Perhaps I laughed to keep the unpleasantness out of the thought. He didn't like it at all.

Since we had skimmed, as I thought, unsuccessfully over the matter of his health there was something else I badly wanted to talk about but was finding it impossible to broach.

Once again I went over to one of the great windows, 'Marvellous how you don't hear much of the passing trains,' I remarked.

He took no notice whatever of that. Switching off the electric fire, which had been unnecessary anyway, he said, 'Come!' and I went with him into the big old-fashioned kitchen, presumably to watch him slice up the meat with the gun beside him on the table. Was I being kept a prisoner . . . or not?

A chopping board stood on the table, with a large French knife beside it and a number of small onions, already peeled. He took the meat out of the refrigerator and sliced it, commenting sourly on the enormous price he had paid for it.

Neither of the servants was present. Encarnita, it seemed, had peeled the onions; they ate 'their own messes' later on. Spaniards like to start their first meal of the day after three o'clock in the afternoon, he said, and they made it last out two hours or so, 'after which they'll set to work with a will to clean out any room.'

I wandered up and down. He nudged the gun a little farther away from him. The kitchen windows looked out across the stable yard and orchard to another stretch of agricultural land behind the house. At last I asked him, point blank, if he were keeping me a prisoner.

He had tied a striped butcher's apron round himself and he straightened up from his task, holding the murderous-looking knife and looking exactly like an old-time butcher. Rainbarrow . . . an anglicized German name. I found myself thinking of the notorious butcher of Hamburg who made his victims into sausages. I'm afraid I have a disorderly mind.

'We have a gentleman's agreement, have we not? You are not exactly detained here but you are here to *think out*, as you yourself put it, what you and your doctor friend are going to put on that death certificate. I appreciate that you have a busy day, and I quite understand that you are doing me a favour by giving me your time. But you see, I'd rather have you here; once you left, you might change your mind; your conscience might get the better of you and you'd go to that Coroner after all. Which would be a big pity.' He was slicing the meat carefully as he talked.

'You're absolutely right there.'

There was a birdcage hanging in front of one of the windows and he went across to it with a fragment of meat which he offered to the brace of love-birds, standing on his toes and making strange sounds like: beep, beep, beep-a-boo. He didn't do it as anyone else would: I can't describe exactly how his movements differed from those of, what for want of a better word one would call a *normal* person; but they were different.

He was a psychopath all right; a psychopath is one who is capable of anti-social behaviour of any kind and lacks the wisdom to appreciate the result of his conduct.

I said, 'It's a marvellous day and I get so little sun; may I be allowed to stroll about in it?'

He hesitated, walking back to the table and picking up the knife again.

'You see, I'm not very hungry; in fact, my appetite isn't what it should be today. The enticing smell of cooking in here and that poor girl upstairs . . .'

'Go on out,' he snapped. 'Your car is locked up but if there's any funny stuff . . .'

'It's all right,' I assured him: 'there won't be. My case is in the hall.'

12 NOON

It all depended upon what he called 'funny stuff'.

I went out of the back door and to give artistic verisimilitude to an otherwise bald and unconvincing narrative, I strolled twice round the house, pausing the first time to look round the stable yard and the second time to examine the old stone trough, fed by a rusted iron pump that was quite picturesque. The tricycle with the basket on the handlebars stood in the open. I felt him watching me from the window. I looked, casually with my hands in my pockets and slowly, at the outbuildings, the old stables and the coach house, in which, I guessed, my car was locked; there was a big well-oiled padlock hanging from the latch. How had he tipped off the Spaniard to take it round the back and lock it away? And where was the key?

Giving a good representation of someone uncertain which way to go, I went back to the drive and started strolling up it slowly and apparently lacking in purpose. I felt sure Rainbarrow found his cooking too engrossing to be able to tear himself from it, even to watch my progress across the park, but I was equally sure either Encarnita or the man would be watching me.

But he had been a lot cleverer than I thought; when I got over the brow of the slope and was sauntering down towards the level crossing I saw the manservant on the other side of the line. What he was doing was laughably artificial: he was scraping away at the surface of the drive with a wide wire rake, removing the weeds. But as the weeds flourished along the drive nearer the house it was clear that the work was only of an emergency order. There had been almost no time since I had left the death chamber when Rainbarrow could have given him instructions, either about the car or about keeping a close watch on the lower part of the drive, so it didn't need any brilliant deduction to understand that there was a certain code of rules between the two for a certain set of circumstances.

If this were a novel instead of a sober statement of fact about what happened three weeks ago, it would be better timed. In an old-fashioned novel the main character never goes out for a stroll to admire the countryside or the sunset, or lies in a garden hammock, or leans over a gate to watch cows, without meeting a key figure of the opposite sex. I yearn to state that I was stooping to examine more closely certain aspects of the level crossing gates, only to find on raising my eyes from my task that a lovely girl was watching me, 'with laughing eyes'. But this was not so.

I walked round the small deserted two-roomed brick bungalow that had been built about the time the railway was laid, to accommodate a gate-keeper for the convenience of those living in the Big House. I had a careful look at the almost brand-new level crossing gates and noticed where the fence had had to be extensively repaired. I could see down-line for a good mile or so but up-line the track disappeared from view round a bend not more than two hundred yards away. I did not have long to wait for a train to pass; a big diesel came almost soundlessly round the bend and as it bore down gave its primitive double hoot. I watched until it had disappeared, then strolled towards the house. At the top of the slope I turned and looked back: the manservant was still industriously scraping the drive and a young woman had just entered the drive gates and was walking up towards him; the bus from the town was driving away along the main road.

I felt quite sure that this was not a normal visitor; people living locally, and not coming by car, would use a bicycle. She was walking quickly and purposefully, not in the way someone would walk who had called casually. I watched her say something to the manservant and I saw them both approaching the level crossing; the man looked both ways, then held open the small pedestrian's gate for her to pass through, evidently telling her to hurry for she nipped across the line pretty quickly and raised her hand by way of thanks.

I strolled on a few yards and sat down on a tree stump, a remnant of the row of beautiful trees which had lined the drive on either side before Mr Rainbarrow had sold them. She hurried towards me and passed without a word or a look. It was not at all what I had expected and I was dumbfounded. She was wearing a plain dark-blue linen town dress, a navy-blue shoulder-bag and flat-heeled shoes; she was smart and slim and businesslike. She was not so much a model type as a high-powered business girl, someone from the BBC or secretary to top pay personnel. All girls are beautiful these days; or else I think they are. Possibly it's my age but I am sure that on the average girls are better-looking than they were in the 'thirties. All I could do was to get up and lumber off after her, feeling extremely silly because it looked as though I had found the drive too much for me and had been resting by the wayside. We were about twenty yards apart by the time she got to the front door. She rang the bell, which was a long narrow iron rod disappearing into the roof of the gothic entrance porch and from the pulling of which no answering ring could be heard from the depths of the house. I advanced upon her helpfully until we were both standing on the immense doormat.

'Have you rung?' I asked.

She nodded, uncommunicative. I officiously tried the door handle; the door was locked. 'Just a minute,' I said and went round to the back door into the kitchen. Rainbarrow was standing with his back to me at the stove and there was an appetizing smell in the kitchen. 'There is a young woman at the front door.'

He swung round, wooden spoon in hand. 'Where is Encarnita?'

'I've no idea!'

He glared at me; I could see the bulge of the gun in his jacket pocket now beneath his striped butcher's apron. But Encarnita had answered the doorbell and came to announce the visitor, in Spanish.

'Christ Almighty,' he swore and tearing off his apron he left the toom.

'Is he going to greet his visitor with that gun in his pocket?' I asked Encarnita. She gave me a long cold look; I was certain she understood what I said but found it more convenient to pretend not to. She said something like: '*No comprendo.*' Spanish is easy to understand if you keep your head and use your imagination.

I stared at her with a feeling of frustration. 'I wish you could tell me more about that young woman's death . . . upstairs.' She cowered against the door and crossed herself. She had understood me perfectly. Encouraged, I went on to tell her a lot more about illegal abortion and the consequences. She understood some of it and the only effect it seemed to have was to make her determined not to utter another word in either English or Spanish. I asked her why the operation was attempted within twelve hours of the girl leaving for Spain this evening but she still cowered and looked at me with the controlled spite of a kicked cat. I felt a big bully as I left her there and pushed open the baize door between the kitchen quarters and the main hall. I went over to my bag, an oasis in a desert of doubt, and stood by it like He protecting his base in a game of tin-can-lurky.

I wondered whether they were in the study or the drawing-room; a well-built house, no sound penetrated the thick closed doors. I thrust my hands in my pockets for want of something to do with them, and waited. After a quarter of an hour or so I was rewarded, the study door opened and the young woman came out in reverse. Rainbarrow was holding the door open for her and she was backing away in protest. She was saying, 'And you can't just push me out like that . . .'

He must have put the pistol back in his desk drawer, I could no longer see the bulge. I didn't move; I was half sitting on the edge of the hall table. I took my hands out of my pockets and folded my arms looking, as I hoped, as though I had the situation in hand. He stood with shoulders hunched and glared at the girl and from what I could see of her back view she was standing up to him, vibrating. There was a tense silence until I cleared my throat. She swung round. If I had only kept quiet I might have learned something.

'If it is your friend Molly O'Dare you are looking for,' I enunciated officiously rather than said, 'I'm afraid there is bad news about her.'

She moved forward a few steps and I put my hand protectively on my bag. 'Who are you?' she asked.

'I'm a doctor, I was called in early this morning to see her.' I ignored the frantic gesticulation that came from Rainbarrow: 'I'm afraid Molly . . . has died,' I said as gently as I could.

I think a tremor shook us both at the roar that came from Rainbarrow. 'God damn it!' he shouted. 'What's happened to you all? This is my house . . . it appears to have been taken over.' He stamped around, in and out of his study, throwing papers about and swearing. That's the sort of thing I mean about losing one's temper; he went so far that he lost our immediate attention.

She came close to me: 'How did she die?'

'That's what I'm here to try to find out; I've been here half the morning.'

'Was she killed or anything?'

'In a way.'

She had gone extremely white or else she was extremely pale anyway, and her mouth was dry.

'I'm staying here as long as I possibly can; another doctor is coming this afternoon; there's something behind all this and I can't for the life of me think what it is.' The storm behind us continued, he was shouting for Encarnita now.

'You can't *send* the police to a house on mere suspicion,' I went on, 'but you can *bring* them. I can smell a police job here and if I stay it may bring them. I'm due at several places this morning and it won't be long before my wife gets anxious at the telephone calls she'll be receiving about where I am. What is worrying me is whether I said where I was coming . . . or not. If I didn't, of course, I'll be here for the rest of my life, which may not be long.'

I looked beyond her, fascinated now because obsessive behaviour of any kind attracts me irresistibly. I murmmured: 'He's got a vile silver safe about the size of a small room; he's already almost had me in there at the point of a gun. The way things are going he should be in a straitjacket by tonight, with luck.'

We were standing fairly close together when I said out of the corner of my mouth, hoping I didn't look as though I were saying anything: 'My name is Lavenham; if you could ring up my wife and tell her I'm here with a madman, it would help. We're the only Lavenhams in the local phone book...'

He stood in front of us, his great shoulders hunched and glared at us: 'You must see... isn't this enough to drive anyone up the pole?'

I said: 'If you could explain why this girl Molly O'Dare was here at all...? Did she come from town in a hired car?'

'Explain? There is no explanation required. Yes, she came in a hired car. Why shouldn't she be visiting her uncle?'

'Uncle?' the new arrival repeated.

'If everything is perfectly simple, Mr Rainbarrow, we would like to know why are you behaving so... excessively?'

'You know, Doctor, everything isn't perfectly simple,' he returned, frowning at me. 'Everything is utterly damnable. You know how things stand between you and me; we're waiting for the arrival of this second doctor; then we can get the death certificate signed and you can be on your way. This young woman here has come from London this morning on the nine-thirty train because, she says, she was "so worried" about Molly O'Dare.'

'I am worried,' she said clearly and slowly, 'because Molly's life was being ruined...'

'Now, now,' he interrupted, 'we don't want any girlish secrets, thank you.'

She stamped her foot: 'You're going to have them, whether you want it or not. Molly's absolutely bewitched by this young man...'

He interrupted again with a loud, mocking laugh: 'What is the point of coming here? I've already told you I've no idea what young man you're talking about.'

'You know perfectly well. He operates from here.'

'*Operates* . . .' He gave an elaborate shrug.

'Why on earth should I have come otherwise, as you said?' She turned to me. 'She was like that advertisement: the girl with lovely eyes, wrapped in a gorgeous mink stole saying she only likes *simple* things. You've seen it, of course?'

I had seen it; the girl portrayed only liked *simple* things such as diamond tiaras, and mink coats, and emerald rings, and Silver Cloud Rolls, and a certain brand of chocolates . . .

'She's never had any money to spend and she says she's always had it drummed into her how poor her family is and so it's gone the other way with her, she's crazy for things that cost money.'

In a burst of internal anger I could see that poor corpse on the bed upstairs as victim of the Advertisers; *she* would want to have some of the things advertised in the glossies: the fifty-guinea pyjamas with ostrich feathers, the Fabergé gold Easter egg, the girl all the plushy advertisers had in mind as they wrote their captions: '. . . *the pyjamas in dreamy mood, fragile and delicate in whispering tea-rose crêpe-de-chine . . . black panther look for girls about the boudoir . . . splendour for prettily pottering about . . .*', the mink coat of which '*every tiny pelt has had to fight its way to the top.*' '*For the Christmas kitten: earrings, One thousand seven hundred pounds . . .*'

I had always wanted to meet the kitten for whom all this talented description was intended, and now I had: upstairs upon the bed and stiffening rapidly by now, unsorrowed, it seemed, and unsung.

1.00 P.M.

He was prowling now, round his hall. I have never seen a wounded bear but I was strongly reminded of one. His face was if possible redder than before and his mouth was still stretched in that curious rictus. I say *still* stretched but that suggests that it was sometimes not and I don't remember ever seeing it other than with that curious unsmile. It is the kind of smile I feel on my own face when I am battling against a fierce north-east wind; not a smile at all – a grimace of endurance.

And about this time I began to wonder if I should telephone to my wife to reassure her that I was *all right.*

But alas, I was very far from being all right.

Still, I thought it best that I should telephone to say that I was all right and that I would probably not be able to get home for lunch and that I would be meeting the train bringing Robin's girl.

I would be obliged to be mysterious because she would immediately ask me what was up and where I was having lunch. She would undoubtedly be more worried if I were to ring than if I didn't; all the same, I thought I had better ring and suggested it; but Rainbarrow said he would rather I didn't.

He stood in front of us. 'You must understand that today is a very important day for me . . .'

'So you have said. Why not tell us in what way?' I interrupted irritably. He ignored the question. He continued: 'It is annoying enough at any time to have a dead girl on one's hands, but today . . . it is absolutely impossible! It's as though the fates had it in for me, upon my word it is! I'm not an easily frightened man, threats don't frighten me, nothing like that. But when I think my luck has changed . . . well, that scares me stiff. So much depends on luck, as Napoleon knew only too well.'

'Quite.' I looked down at the girl standing by my side and wondered how often he had a dead girl on his hands; she was staring at Rainbarrow in alarm.

'I want that body out of this house as quickly as possible and since I can't get in touch with the undertakers without having your death certificate in order, I have to detain you here until it is.'

'But surely – ' the girl hesitated – 'that's Molly's parents' business, isn't it? Her mother is on her way to London now. She flew from Ireland last night.' There was a long vibrating pause. 'I sent for her. Molly was in trouble and so I sent for her. Well, why not? I share a flat with her daughter and I am her friend. I was responsible for her in a way, she's a lot younger than I am anyway . . .' She started to cry a little: 'God! I keep using the present tense; I can't get it into my head that she's dead . . .'

But there was always food, it seemed, to comfort Mr Rainbarrow's sad heart. Apparently remembering his veal stew, he hurried through the swing door back to the kitchen and I let the girl cry for a few minutes. It looked as though it would be simple to open the front door and leave the house in a normal way. I knew I should not be allowed to pass the manservant on the drive but I saw no reason why she should not leave. I shook her arm gently. 'Listen, whatever-your-name-is, why don't you hop it now? I should.'

'I've only just come,' she wailed.

'I should disappear if I were you.'

'No fear!' she returned emphatically.

'Well, if you don't mind my saying so, you damn well must go! I do assure you that there's going to be a big row here later on. You won't be wanted and you're much better out of it.'

'I'm Molly's friend. I'm not even sure she's dead yet. How do I know you're telling me the truth?'

'If you must know, your friend died as the result of an illegal operation, performed by someone else. I'm not sure when she died but I was called in early this morning. She was dead when I got here and for a time Rainbarrow accused me of killing her. It was a bad mistake; I think he saw that almost at once. It made me suspicious immediately. If they had met me in distress and told me what had happened I'd have had to report it, of course, but I wouldn't have immediately jumped to the conclusion that I was dealing with a bunch of criminals. And when he got out his revolver and threatened me with it . . . well, that was it. They're all in it, all three.'

'Three?'

'Rainbarrow and the two Spanish servants.'

'Then you haven't met Micky?'

'Who the hell is he?'

There was no reply.

1.15 P.M.

She said her name was Nell Fitton. She was a State Registered nurse and while taking her midwifery course at a London hospital she had a small flat and when the friend with whom she shared it got married, she advertised for another girl to take her place. Molly O'Dare was the one she chose because 'she was so nice'. They had shared the flat for the past two years and there had been none of that irritability that sometimes occurs between girls sharing a flat; Molly had been consistently nice all the way along and Nell had grown very fond of her.

Having no family of her own, Nell had gone home to Ireland for Christmas with Molly and met her family, an ageing and crotchety earl, his son, due to inherit, married with four children, and Lady Lakeland, Molly's mother, a wholly charming person but overworked. She had had a 'wonderful time'.

But before long Molly had become discontented with her job as typist to a lawer in Chancery Lane and had gone to a place where they trained good-looking girls as models. It was probably that, Nell thought, which had increased her taste for clothes and jewels and all the luxuries that a girl was supposed to crave. She had taken commissions modelling underwear and that, as everyone knew (except me), was considered a comparatively low-grade job. She had sworn never to mention it to *anyone* because, Molly said, if her parents got to know they would immediately order her home and she would have to go, because she was like that.

I would probably have learned more but Rainbarrow came back, with his jacket off, and asked us into the kitchen. He was evidently not going to leave us together for long.

Encarnita, mournful and haggard-eyed, was laying the table in a small room next to the kitchen. He told us to sit down and put a newly-opened bottle of sherry before us. I poured out a glass for Nell Fitton.

'Drink it,' I suggested, 'it will buck you up a bit.'

But I left her crying into her handkerchief and went into the kitchen where Rainbarrow was stirring the thick creamy sauce for the veal. He ignored my presence; there was a greedy glitter in his eye and I wondered if, had circumstances been different, he would have been preparing the meal for himself and Molly, or perhaps simply for himself only.

There might have been nothing more important in heaven and earth as he bent over the small wooden bowl in which he had chopped parsley; no bacteriologist on the verge of discovering penicillin, or scientist about to split the atom, could have put more eager concentration into his movements.

He told me to stir the sauce in its small saucepan and keep the flame low; he was going to make a quick telephone call and when he returned he would put the two egg yolks and cream into the sauce, pour it over the meat and the meal would be ready. 'But don't stop stirring,' he said as he left the room.

I did, of course; I followed him along the kitchen passage and from the baize door watched him shut himself into his study. I pressed my ear against the three-inch thick wood and could hear nothing. I returned to the kitchen where the sauce had stuck in a layer to the bottom of the pan; as I stirred it the small pieces came adrift;

they were burnt and brown.

He was cross when he returned five minutes later, but not very, he didn't waste his anger; he looked at me as though he thought me a half-wit; snatched the pan up, peered into it, sighed and shrugged his shoulders, sieved it and added the egg yolks.

'I've been telephoning to your wife,' he said as he peered down into the mixture. 'I told her you had a difficult case and would not be home for lunch.'

I asked him if he happened to mention to her where I was. He raised his head and looked at me with stretched mouth, telling me not to try to be clever. He added that he thought it better to ring and when I asked him why, he did not answer. Nor did he deign to answer such a stupid question when I asked if he had mentioned who was calling her. I said I would have liked to have a word with her myself and he said that he was sure I would and that I would have plenty of time for that when I got home this evening, with a nice bundle of clean fivers in my bag. That would be, I said, *if* I got home and without looking up again he added that that, of course, would be up to me.

He put the meat into a beautiful early Sheffield plate entrée dish, poured the creamy sauce over it, put on the lid and slipped it into the oven. Then we went into the small room next door and sat down at the table; he poured himself a glass of sherry and pushed the bottle across the table, telling us to help ourselves. Nell had put away her handkerchief and her tears had ceased to flow but she was looking pinched and wretched.

In anticipation of food his mood was expansive. Leaning across the table, he assured her that he did not want to make an enemy of her but he did not find it easy to be sure who, in this world, was motivated by genuine kindness and who by miserable poke-nose curiosity. One thing he could not stand was people who poked and pried; he'd had quite enough of that sort of thing when he had lived in the town, many years ago. He'd had an old curiosity shop, the doctor here would remember it. Well, the gossip that he had had to endure! Just because he was a bachelor and one who carried on his business in second-hand goods, it seemed he had to be chewed to bits by the whole town. As soon as he'd had enough money saved up (and it wasn't so easy in those days, my dear) he had moved out of town, and he had chosen a house that was as isolated as he could find. His visitors could come and go as they liked, he was thankful to say; he was not overlooked; his own comings and his goings too were unobserved, and thus he was able to obtain the peace that was every man's right. 'At Dedend, as they call it,' he sneered.

And furthermore, he said, that was why he had foreign servants; it was a pleasure to have a woman about the place who could not speak, or rather he should say could not *talk*. He paid them enough to make it worth their while being isolated, at a dead end, and on their days off, once a week, he sent them by taxi to the station where they got cheap day tickets to London. And they found a day in London much more attractive than a day spent in the little local town.

Then he gave a thumbnail portrait of himself, his idea of his own image. Starting: 'You see, my dear – ' I was evidently not included in this avuncular dissertation – 'I have always been an individualist, I don't bow to convention. I do say, think and *eat* – ' he gave me a short dagger-look – 'what I like. I believe in freedom of movement and in a small town it is impossible. I'm an eccentric and I'm proud of it. I know perfectly well what they say: "There's funny old Mr Rainbarrow on his tricycle," but I don't care. I'm a man who lives his life the way he wants, and enjoys it.' He drained his sherry glass in self-satisfaction.

'But do you?' I asked contentiously.

'I most certainly do.' He belched very slightly as he poured out another glass of the excellent Bristol Milk.

'Then today is one of those awkward days when things aren't going the way you want!'

'Don't worry,' he replied, smacking his lips from the sherry, 'I've always had things the way I want.'

I noted that his self-confidence ebbed and flowed but not necessarily in direct ratio to his alcoholic intake.

'Nell Fitton,' I said, 'have you ever heard of Mr Rainbarrow before?' I was sitting beside him and turned to watch his face as I asked the question. He was looking down at the table thoughtfully and as I spoke his smile seemed suddenly to drop off, like a pair of spectacles, and for a few moments he stared at the place on the table where it seemed to have fallen.

'Yes, I have. Molly has been away to Spain twice before with Micky and both times she came down here first; that's how I heard of this place where Micky's uncle lives. And that's why I've come here today; I thought I'd catch her, she isn't going until tonight. Wasn't, I mean. Micky has built a marvellous block of flats near Torremolinos; he has to go over there a lot to see things are okay. She was flying tonight and he was following her tomorrow; they never went on the same plane . . .'

'What a dreadful little gossip you are,' Rainbarrow barked; his smile was back in place now.

'Tell me,' I said urgently, 'have you met Molly's uncle before?'

She looked bewildered. Rainbarrow called Encarnita to serve the meal. 'I met a lot of her relatives when I was at her home,' she said.

'But this old gentleman?'

She shook her head.

'Is he *not* Molly's uncle?'

'Micky's uncle,' she said, 'but Molly called him "Uncle".' I looked across at him but he appeared not to have heard.

'I see.' In the bustle of serving I was thinking hard. A week ago, I couldn't remember what day, a young man with an Irish accent and strange haircut had been among the waiting patients at our surgery on one of my mornings. He had stayed until everyone else had left and I, thinking he was a salesman, had spoken to him in the waiting-room on my way out to the car. He had asked to have a word with me in private and when, back in my consulting-room, I had heard what he wanted, I had bustled him out as firmly and quickly as possible saying that I was surprised that he should ask a general practitioner such a question. He had the impertinence to say that he thought anyone would do anything for money, if there was enough offered. It would be like winning the pools, he added. He was quite a talkative chap, the gift of the gab and the Irish blarney kind of thing. He said the whole idea of coming to a respectable general practitioner was common sense; it would be done properly, no hole-and-corner stuff, and no risks attached.

To be asked to terminate a pregnancy is something that happens fairly frequently so it did not make much of an impression on me. I hustled him off and I hadn't given the thing a thought since, except that now I did remember, as I started up my car, thinking: 'Pity I couldn't take the Micky out of him!' Not exactly an epoch-making thought but a reminder.

A plate of delicious-smelling food was put down in front of each of us but I wasn't going to be the first to start.

Nell Fitton raised her blotchy eyes to Rainbarrow. 'Where *is* Micky, anyway?'

Rainbarrow took a heaped forkful of food and shovelled it into his mouth with greedy appreciation. 'How should I know?' he said disgustingly through the food.

'You must know...'

He took no more notice but gave his attention to the meal.

'You know perfectly well where he is. Don't tell me he's run off in fright because Molly's... died? That's it, isn't it? Tell me, tell me...' She banged her fists on the table, playing a tattoo, so that the cutlery jangled in time to her beats. 'You know Micky can't do a damn thing without you, you *run* the poor beast; you possess him. Sometimes I think he is longing to get right from you and be on his own. I think that's why he would always rather be in Spain than here. The block of flats can run itself really but he stays there to be away from you. I think he *hates* you...' Her voice had risen now, slightly hysterical.

He stood up, towering over her, roaring at her to be quiet, that he must have his meals in peace. If I had been sitting on the other side of the table I would have put my arm round her to steady her; as it was I got on quietly with my meal, which was excellent. I haven't tasted a *blanquette de veau* since I had it when my wife and I were last in Paris ages ago in that little restaurant near Les Halles, which specializes in pigs' trotters.

The telephone bell rang and he left the room bumping clumsily from side to side in his haste; the ring was very loud indeed and I realized that from the study there was an auxiliary bell outside, in the kitchen passage.

Nell Fitton was crying again and in the comparative lull I told her to try not to get worked up: 'You're in a much stronger position if you don't,' I said, and went on to tell her she should try to eat something, it was excellent. She said that the idea of eating now was absolutely disgusting to her and I said I could see her point and I hoped she would forgive me if I ate because I was going to need some sustenance if I was to cope with the present situation. At the moment, I told her, I was in the finding-out position, marking time; the longer I stayed the more I was finding out. I was hoping that before I left the house I would have everything tied up. 'Possibly even the villain himself,' I added, hoping to make her smile.

What on earth I would do if Robin's girl were not coming, I did not have time to think. At the moment I was not thinking of her as Robin's girl so much as another doctor; I needed a colleague badly. Apart from other considerations, I wanted someone with whom to discuss Rainbarrow's mental state. That he was 'mad' I had no doubt, but the word covers a number of conditions themselves divided and sub-divided and to call him a psychopath was as unspecific as to say that some animal is a dog. *What kind of dog* is the interesting point.

Rainbarrow came back into the room. He was holding a newspaper, folded back at the racing page. He sat down and continued to eat his lunch with the paper across his knees, glancing down from time to time, taking no notice of us.

'What time did you say your friend would be arriving from London, Doctor?' he asked, though it had not been mentioned yet.

'The two-fifteen. There is plenty of time before I go to meet the train.'

He gave a short sharp laugh. 'Come off it,' he said, 'you don't think I'm as big a mug as that, do you? You'll have to give me a description of him. Paco will do the meeting.'

'I would have liked to discuss the case with my colleague in my car on our way back here.'

'Of course you would, Doc, of course you would; but I'm not taking any risks.'

Rainbarrow was having a second helping, which I had refused. I pushed my chair back from the table and said discursively: 'You know, you're not behaving like a country gentleman at all; you're behaving like one of the criminal class. It strikes me most forcibly.'

'What do you call the criminal class?'

'Those people about whom Parliament talk when they discuss the abolition of hanging. Not ordinary men and women, because on the whole, ordinary men and women are not criminals. They do not wish to acquire money by any means other than legal ones, they do not scheme and plot to obtain money by illegal means. And they don't kill people . . .'

'Look, what the hell are you talking about?'

'You heard. I suggested that you are behaving like a criminal; you suspect people's motives.'

'*I suspect yours* because you're indignant about a criminal act which seems to have occurred in my house. I'm asking you to overlook it and you have refused, so far.'

He pushed his empty plate away, got up and went into the kitchen to make coffee. I followed him and stood around while he made it. I looked out of the window, it was still a glorious day. Miss Cloverly-ffane would be having a splendid time out on the river with her friend; my wife would be working hard in her kitchen, preparing our celebration dinner for our guest, she would be making some delicious festive pudding and would probably be relieved that I had not come home to lunch. The morning woman would have made-up the guest-room bed and my wife would have put flowers on the dressing-table and a set of clean towels in the guest bathroom. My black Labrador would be lying on the front doorstep, floppy mouth down on his fat paws, his brown eyes watching the bees among the dwarf campanula. He has always admitted the bees were there by special permission but if any of them got unruly he would soon deal with them.

Rainbarrow put the coffee-pot down on the tray and went across to his birds: '*Beep*-a-doop, doop, doop, doop ...' he chirped. There was a quality of nightmare about it, a fragment of something that sticks in the memory so that years later it is still there and gives the same feeling of remembered horror. I shall think now and again of that vast man and his unnatural tenderness for his love-birds as long as I live.

2.00 P.M.

It was a gruesome little gathering over coffee in the drawing-room, having the outward appearance of a social occasion and being, in fact, anything but.

While he got the brandy I tried to cheer up Nell Fitton by pointing out the white marble caryatids holding up the chimney piece. 'Who do you think did what to whom?' I asked but there was no answering smile. As a talking point I couldn't leave them alone; I gave a little dissertation on the visual arts of the late Victorian era to which she showed little appearance of listening. 'And anyway,' I said, 'this couple want a good scrub.' I touched the woman lightly and she wobbled. 'Typical!' I jeered. 'Gimcrack . . .'

He was coming in through the door as I demonstrated the wobble to Nell Fitton; absently holding the tray at a slant, with one hand he snatched at the brandy bottle to save it but the glasses slithered off and shattered on the floor. There was no shouting or ranting this time but as I stooped to help pick up the fragments I was aware that he was shaking. His voice quivered, too, as he said in a shrill treble: 'Admiring my ornaments, were you?'

Nell Fitton could not be bothered to help us tidy up; she sat hunched and self-absorbed. Solicitously helpful, I went back to the dining-room with him to get three more brandy glasses and soon we were all three sitting with our VSOP and between sips he was doing the wandering minstrel's song in breath-whistling again and I was staring at the white marble angry female with the torn dress.

'They didn't go with the house, then?' I remarked casually.

'No. No. They came from my old home,' he lied. 'You're interested in Victoriana, then, Dr Lavenham?'

'Yes, indeed. Don't you remember the jokey cheese dish my wife and I bought from your shop, many years ago?'

He looked straight across at me and the stretched lips and cold eyes gave me the shivers. 'I can't remember all my customers, all those years ago.'

'No, quite. But I thought you might remember the cheese dish; it is a model of the Albert Hall, we use it all the time, even if there is only a two-inch-square bit of "mousetrap" left.'

But it was no good, I couldn't get the party going. We sat like three unacquainted people in a British Rail waiting-room except that as I drank the excellent brandy my optimism rose. This was an adventure, I thought excitedly; the only one I have ever had that wasn't connected with warfare.

The brandy must have taken his mind off whatever was concerning him because he now gave his attention to Nell Fitton.

'You're an impertinent little thing,' he said pleasantly, 'daring to say that my own nephew ... what was it? ... *hates* me.' He shook his head: 'Not nice, not nice. How well do you know him?'

'Well!'

'Oh, he's a one, he is!' Rainbarrow drooled in a way that gave me the shivers. 'He has a way with him and he's a real one for the girls. I remember telling him, when he came in that jazzy car – (you'll have seen it) I said *you* don't need a car like that, man; you've got everything a girl wants anyway!'

'Stop it,' Nell Fitton shouted irritably, 'stop it, I can't

stand it! How you can talk like that . . .'

'But seriously, my dear –' he leaned forward, elbows on his great thighs, brandy glass cupped in both hands to warm it – 'it would be better if you left. As it is, I have one unwanted guest in my house today . . . it is really absurd that I should have to put up with two; you're one too many. I must allow Dr Lavenham to stay for an hour or so longer, but I don't have to keep *you* with me.'

'If you do turn me out of the house before Micky comes I'll go straight to the police!'

He raised his eyebrows until they nearly touched his ridiculous hair. 'Now really, Miss Fitton! What do you hope to gain by staying here?'

'. . . And after that I'll go back home and tell her mother everything . . .' A slightly childish recession, I considered. 'She'll be in London probably by now, looking for us both.'

Yes, she is entirely redundant, I thought, but why on earth is she rubbing it in?

'I shouldn't be surprised if you're in love with Micky yourself,' Rainbarrow said nastily. 'I've never met a woman who knew him who wasn't yet.'

'Of course I'm not!' she returned feebly. 'He was Molly's friend, not mine.'

He gave his terrible whinnying laugh. ' "The World's Sweetheart", boy or girl? Eh? I don't think it's a bad name for our Micky. Well, if it will help at all I can tell you he won't be here so there isn't any point in your waiting to see him.'

'I'm not, I'm not . . .' Nell stammered hopelessly. But I could see that he had something; if he was too clever for me, he was much too clever for Nell Fitton. I wondered for a few minutes whether he had won and she had decided to go but after a time I decided she was staying doggedly; she seemed to have put herself into a shockingly dangerous position and she was fully aware of it but there was a kind of desperate persistence about her as though she felt that nothing worse than what had already happened could happen to her.

Poor Nell Fitton! I felt sorry for her, though she was tall and self-possessed, yet she seemed all adrift; her looks belied her worried self and as I think of her now, hunched in her chair, holding her brandy glass with one hand and with the other running her fingers over her face, I feel I could and should have done something about her, but even now, in the light of everything I know, I still ask myself... what? Long, long ago someone ought to have told her to come in out of the wet; who was I to tell her now and what possible hope would I have had of getting her to take my advice?

Even at that stage of the day, I now see, I was not taking things seriously; it was as though I had wandered inadvertently into a mystery story; I had to stay and read to the end; and somewhere, right at the back of my mind, wherever that is, I had the pleasurable feeling that I was going to enjoy recounting it all to my wife when I got home tonight. I suppose that when nothing was actually happening (and the gun remained out of sight), I was forming phrases in my mind with which I was going to thrill her: 'You simply wouldn't believe how evil he looked... et cetera, et cetera, et cetera.'

In the end I told my wife very little; it was all too real. She is happy and gay and somehow or other I didn't want her to know about that 'funny old Mr Rainbarrow', about whom she and Robin would giggle together when Robin was small and they encountered him out shopping.

Encarnita and Paco, Paco and Encarnita: key characters

yet background figures; I cannot bring them into focus however much I may want to because I saw too little of them. And yet they added up, in the end, to more than the original sum.

Encarnita: she had blonde (dyed of course) hair; she was fat, with wonderfully thin ankles and wrists and beautiful delicate hands. She was a whole, round (literally) person with bruised flesh about her eyes and a tragic look and I know without having actually experienced it that she was extremely light on her feet, probably a marvellous dancer. She was utterly devoted to, a part of, Paco.

And Paco? He must also remain at a distance: slim-hipped, low-browed, watchful-eyed, the sort whose steady eyes keep on looking into yours while the steady hand is in the sugar bowl; wise beyond his years, completely aware of 'the shadow of our night, Envy and calumny and hate and pain'; fully alive to the importance of being rich; he accepted without question the wicked world. He probably thought it a pity that here one was so devoted to riches (wealth we would call it) that we would go to any lengths to be rich; probably to the end he would be convinced that all Englishmen were so, but he was not indifferent to the rich rewards that could come his way. There is a point at which a Spaniard will stop, a limit beyond which it would anger his God if he went; Paco was typical: he could lie and cheat just so far . . . and no farther. The Spaniard is terribly afraid of and impressed by death; except in self-defence, *crime passionel* or madness, he does not, as a rule, murder; he is appalled by it.

These reflections on the Spanish couple occur at this particular point because, though I had seen so little of them, soon I was to see nothing at all. Only hear.

2.30 P.M.

Sitting in the drawing-room with Rainbarrow and Nell Fitton, I could see the sun streaming down on the hot gravel outside the closed windows; brandy glass in hand, I was aware of, rather than listened to, the conversation between them; my attention was almost wholly absorbed by my thoughts regarding the wobbling marble woman. The conversation became more sharp and rancorous; I usually cease to take any notice when people get to the childish I did . . . you didn't . . . I *did* . . . you *didn't* . . . stage, but thinking back I know it was about the ubiquitous *Micky*, whether he was – or was not – coming, with Nell Fitton asserting over and over again that he must be because Molly had *said so* and Rainbarrow truculently denying it. And with part of my mind I was looking forward to seeing the fabulous Micky once again, against his weird background.

After a long pulsating pause in the argument, Nell Fitton burst out again in vigorous protest: she knew how much Molly had made at her modelling and it was nothing like the amount of money she had to spend. She knew that each time Molly returned from Spain she brought a lot of money with her. She was generous with it, she would buy things for other people as well as for herself. The point was, she explained, that she (Nell) was not exactly unobservant; that money hadn't been come by in any normal way. She'd been thinking it over and it seemed perfectly clear to her that Micky was involved in one of the many ways in which people can make money other than by working for it. His new block of flats was conveniently near Gibraltar . . . any sort of smuggling could be going on and Molly could be used for it. They didn't have Guardia Civil every hundred yards or so along the southern coast of Spain for nothing!

Rainbarrow sipped his brandy gingerly and his comments were a series of short hard barks of a kind vaguely resembling laughter. Silly girl, silly girl, he called her, over-imaginative, hysterical. Molly was Micky's mistress and Micky made money out of the rents of his flats in Spain; naturally he gave Molly money to bring home; many of his clients paid in English and American currency, what could be more normal than giving some of it to his best girl? Making trouble, he called it, and simply through jealousy; if she were in the position that poor Molly had been in, she would not think of it, accept gratefully and shed her light as Molly had done.

He sounded fairly relaxed but anyone could have sensed the man's tension; he seemed, all the time, to be listening and often he got up and walked across to the windows. He was waiting for something, he had been waiting for something all day. He stood in front of her, looking down with his everlasting smile. If she really thought Micky was coming, he suggested, would it not be a good thing to do something about her face?

'Oh, you cruel beast!' she cried. 'What does it matter about my face with poor Molly up there . . .' and once again she wept silently into her snarled-up handkerchief.

'I'll show you to the "Ladies"',' he said, lightly facetious; I could hardly believe my ears; the one thing I wanted was to be alone in the room and it was the one thing I was sure he did not want. Was he actually going out with her on this mere tiny frivolous pretext?

Perhaps she really did wish to visit the 'Ladies'', for

presently they both left the room and I leaped across to the fireplace and prised the outraged marble female from her moorings. She was far from slim; two screws emerged from her spine at strategic points north and south with a foot-long space between them which contained a very neat, tiny, narrow wall safe, flush with the wall, completely hidden by her marble draperies. It was by no means the first time she had been pulled away from the wall, the holes into which the screws fitted bled dust and had become slightly jagged round the edges, the packing round the screws would have been entirely adequate in keeping the figure back in place if it had been renewed but, with continuous pulling in and out of their holes, both had disintegrated, becoming frayed and fragmentary. I pushed her back home and felt like putting out my tongue at her marvellously curly lips and the thin Greek nose down which she looked with such disdain.

When I heard the first shot I was so far removed from reality that in my disordered mind's eye I saw myself start back with an exaggerated gesture: 'Hark, what was that I heard?' But with the second shot I came down to earth and, in the dark looking-glass that was part of the chimney piece, I stared at my own grey-flannel face, flaccid with horror.

Looking back to immortal moments like this, it is impossible to say how long things took, how many minutes or seconds, with any degree of accuracy. I know I walked across the room and opened the door into the hall, where I saw Rainbarrow standing by the table; he had the familiar gun, in front of him an old-fashioned wooden housemaid's box in which was shoe-cleaning tackle; he was smearing brown polish on a pair of walking shoes and breath-whistling: 'a wandering minstrel I, a thing of shreds and patches . . .'

2.40 P.M.

Was it a gun *I* had heard? Did someone fire two shots? I didn't say that, or anything like it, because I knew; it is not my custom to imagine that I hear gunshots. If I ever had much imagination, it has been rusted by disuse long ago. A little imagination is a good thing in a doctor but an active one is a disadvantage; I found it much more convenient to work on sober facts.

Within the last four minutes, perhaps less, Rainbarrow had fired one shot: he was now cleaning his shoes and I could clearly see on the front of one wrist the pulse beating slowly and regularly; nor was he in the slightest degree out of breath.

I was frightened. I was, in fact, shaking inwardly with sheer fright and as I was now firmly gummed to my bag I was thankful I had picked it up from the hall, because clutching the old familiar handle concealed the trembling and gave me a feeble strength to simulate unconcern. Through dry lips I made the all-time banal remark: 'Cleaning your shoes?'

He grunted. 'Um! The last Spaniard I had was an exhibition shoe-cleaner; he'd whistle a tune all the time, always the same tune, and throw his brushes in the air between movements of polishing. A juggler-shoe-cleaner. But Paco! I've never been able to get him to do them properly.'

He was certainly not out of breath, he had plenty of it for talking.

'My mother always said you can tell a gentleman by the

state of his shoes,' and he allowed his glance to travel lightly over my own somewhat dusty suède ones. He ran his brush across a shoe and, hypnotized, I watched the polish gradually appear while measuring up his physique against my own and trying to assess the result of a physical attack upon him. I am afraid too many years of refraining from battery has told upon me; to assault someone, you have to have an irresistible urge to do so and I hadn't. I simply stood beside him until he had polished both shoes, stuffed the materials into the box.

'Where is Nell Fitton?' I croaked.

'Gone. I persuaded her that it was better to go home and she left just before you came out of the drawing-room.'

Did he really think I hadn't heard?

I went to the front door and tried it; it opened and I stood outside, staring ahead. She would not have had time to go up the drive and disappear from sight during the shoe-cleaning pantomime . . . but I was sure she hadn't. And as I stood there I was again shocked by a bitter screech a sound as old as time when the ice-age woman stood in the entrance to her cave and yelled for her mate.

'Paco . . . Paco . . . *Paco!*'

A Spanish woman from the doors of her hut will scream for her husband to come home from the mountain-top, eight miles away.

Apart from Paco, still on guard, I could have run for it, down the mile-long drive and out into the main road where I could have thumbed a lift for the nearest police station two miles down the road. I'm not much of a sprinter but I might have made it. Looking back, I can think of no good reason why I didn't do that except that I didn't want to get shot. I knew that there were now two dead girls in the house and that seemed to fill my mind to the exclusion of any escape attempt. I'm certain now that at the time I didn't consider it for a moment.

'*Paco!*' The sound scraped the lining of my skull.

I turned back to the hall; he was putting the shoe-cleaning box away in an elaborately carved rug-chest. I couldn't take my eyes off him; I was sure that he had led Nell Fitton out of the drawing-room, into some other room in the house, had threatened her with his gun: 'Go away or I'll shoot.' She had refused to *go* and he had shot her, as he would have shot me for refusing to *stay*. He had left her dead and returned to the hall to clean his shoes with as much unconcern as a farmer would go out into the yard and wring the neck of a cock. But the farmer would at least tie the cock's legs together at once and hang it from a nail. Rainbarrow hadn't had time to do anything much; had he escorted her to the 'Ladies'' as he called it and shot her as he pushed her inside? I saw the door in the corner of the hall, I went across and looked inside. He saw me.

I followed him into the drawing-room, where he took up his brandy glass and drained it. So he did at least feel he needed that spot of revival. His looking at his watch was like a nervous twitch but this time he said: 'Isn't it about time we thought of meeting this other doctor friend of yours?' And he added hurriedly: 'Paco will go to the station, of course. I assume you will lend him your car; I haven't one, as you know.' He jerked his head in the direction of the Spanish screech and said, so unnecessarily that I would have laughed if I had been in laughing mood: 'Encarnita is calling him in now.'

You filthy black-hearted killer! No, I hadn't said it; I was still alone and silent in the secret world of Tom Lavenham. From the window I watched Paco running back towards the house, carrying his rake.

'Come,' Rainbarrow beckoned me and it was clear that he was not going to let me out of his sight for long; we went back to the kitchen where I sat on the edge of the table and he beep-beep-beeped at his love-birds. He let them both perch on his forefinger and drew them out of the cage proudly to show me, like a child. He held their beaks against his cheek, against his mouth, he stroked the top of their colourful heads with his other forefinger. I did not see any gun.

'No flying about today,' he murmured tenderly as he put them carefully back.

'If anyone is going to the station they had better get a move on,' I suggested surlily.

He went briskly along the stone passage to the back door and called Paco in from the yard. The Spaniards both entered, as close together as it is possible for any two people to move who are not actually dancing. They looked as though they had each had a blow on the solar plexus. Since it was evidently Paco who, earlier on, had taken my little car round to the garage, there was no wasting words about the key (which I always leave in the car because I've no time to fiddle around locking and unlocking) and whether he could drive or not, but he tried to get out of it by saying that he had no driving licence. Rainbarrow snapped irritably that he must drive carefully so that there would be no occasion to produce his licence.

'If you will give a short description of your friend, Doctor, Paco won't need to waste any time.'

'A Chinese,' I said vaguely. 'You can tell her that I am unable to meet her myself because of an urgent case but that I would be grateful for her help with the case.'

Rainbarrow swung round: 'Her!'

'A lady doctor,' I murmured.

'Lady doctor,' he snorted. 'Women, women everywhere! Women shouldn't be doctors . . .' I thought of telling Paco that if he should see my wife, in a grey pickup, also meeting her, he could tell her where I was but dismissed the idea as too full of complications, for one thing – my wife's own car was having a maintenance at six thousand miles. He stared back at me, stony-faced, and I heard Rainbarrow booming: '. . . a woman should be either on her back or on her knees. A woman doctor, I wouldn't have one near me! And Chinese at that!'

I looked at the clock. It would be twenty minutes' drive to the main-line station in my Mini. If Paco was late it would give time for my wife to collect the girl. It was more possible, though, that in my absence she had sent the local car-hire because, being Clover's day out, she would be unwilling to leave the house.

I said I would very much like to drive to the station since Paco's driving was in doubt, but I knew Rainbarrow would not let me. What he did allow was that since they were not on any account to have an accident, Paco had better ask 'the Chinese woman' to drive my Mini back here.

Much relieved I left it at that.

'Are you playing fair, Lavenham? Is this woman a qualified doctor, and *Chinese*, did you say?' He came close to me, his lips stretched and his face apparently enduring a strong cold wind. His head back, he peered at me closely, through the bottom part of his bi-focals.

'A qualified woman doctor, and yes, Chinese!' I shouted as though he were deaf.

'I didn't expect that,' he grumbled, 'when you said you had a doctor friend arriving after luncheon; upon my word I didn't!'

'What the hell difference does it make? She's every bit as capable of examining the body and giving her opinion as to the cause of death as I am.'

'My God!' he started wagging his finger at me most offensively, 'if there has been any trickery, if there's any funny stuff . . .'

'There hasn't, I assure you.'

'You won't leave this house alive . . .'

'I can quite believe that!'

He had half turned away but now he swung back and demanded in a roaring crescendo what the hell I meant by that.

'I have one main ambition at present and that is to leave this house alive, I promise you. It is perfectly obvious that I can't get either of my colleagues in on it; this doctor seems to be an absolute godsend, for want of a better word, as far as you're concerned. It is the only answer to your problem. Otherwise you're going to have to do a lot of explaining.

'A Chinese lady doctor,' he mused, 'upon my word!'

'So what!' I yelled nervily. 'Would you rather have a one-legged Portuguese fortune-teller?'

He drew back alarmed and I mooched across to the hall window and stood with my back to him until I heard a familiar sound and saw my white Mini disappearing up the drive with Paco, alone, in it. Then I opened my bag, overstuffed and ridiculously untidy, and started another elaborate examination of the contents.

3.45 P.M.

Papa Ah Mee, Juniper's father, is a mandarin and, peeling away the mystique that covers that word, one learns that he is a banker in Peking. Many Chinese mandarins live in modern houses and flats but the house of her father that Juniper has described to me was built on the stringent rules of Chinese geomancy, that is, from the figures derived by the throwing down of a handful of earth upon the ground; all, one might say, at sixes and sevens, and with a random charm about it; a pink house standing in the grey dust of a Peking street not far from the Tartar wall. Fragile as a pagoda, it is built round a courtyard with a pine tree in the centre and bitterly draughty in winter when the icy winds blow down from Siberia.

Though in the China of today the dead are not as important as they were, in many households they are still held in great respect and Papa Ah Mee has bought himself a splendid lacquered coffin and stored it in a temple against the day when it will be needed. He has three sons, two of whom are in the bank and one a doctor. Juniper, the youngest child, followed her brother's example and studied medicine, taking her degree in Peking. The brothers are married and many children swarm about the pink house near the Tartar wall. This is probably the reason for Juniper's decision to specialize in pædiatrics and she has been in the children's department of Trinity Hospital for two years.

In the short time I have known her, she has told me

many charming things about her people and in future she will tell me many more, so that when I see photographs of expressionless flat-faced men and women in their padded jackets, members of the People's Commune, I shall try to remember that she told me that her father's gardener places dry tea-leaves in the lotus flower before it closes at sundown and in the morning, as the flower opens, he removes them and later the family drink lotus-flavoured tea. I shall try to remember the Chinese have been like that much longer than they are like this.

Though she has not said so, I gather, from all she has told me, that Papa Ah Mee is extremely rich, or was, because at present there exists an arrangement which is quite beyond my comprehension by which he shares his business with the Communists on a basis of two to one, he having the lesser share.

'My father is supremely intelligent,' she said, 'and he was strongly against my coming to England. Deep down there is still a feeling that his daughter is among "foreign devils". But as one of my uncles was at the London School of Economics, he came to plead with my father and he at last allowed me to come.' When she saw me smiling she guessed that the word 'allowed' amused me.

'But you see,' she murmured, 'he is my honourable parent and I could not go against his wishes.' I wondered if their children would think of his Juniper and our Robin as their 'honourable parents'.

Knowing what I now know about her and looking back to those first minutes at Rainbarrow's house, I find my own immediate reaction to her quite grotesque.

It seemed hours and hours before they returned from the station, the Spaniard and Dr Ah Mee: Rainbarrow, like a lion, restlessly pacing his cage and I, arms wrapped one over the other, sulkily slumped in a chair in the drawing-room. And finally, when she did arrive, my heart sank with a thump which could have been heard several feet away.

She was like a reed as she sat at the driving wheel, the sort that hasn't any stamina at all and gets shaken, not to say broken, with the wind. She was dressed in a silvery-green *cheong-sam* with a high collar and a slit up the side from Dan to Beersheba, showing a leg slim as that of a robin. She was carrying a kind of basketwork shoulder bag and wearing a pair of minute white high-heeled sandals.

The disgusting habit of binding their feet! I absurdly thought (Chinese women's feet haven't been bound for years), and I also looked at her hips and thought how little room there would be between them for my grandchildren to grow. She simply had no figure at all and her face was, inevitably, ivory-coloured and quite, quite expressionless. Her eyes . . . in common with everyone else, I think a woman's greatest asset is her eyes and Juniper's eyes were and still are (though now I love her, eyes and all) almost lashless and poky.

I had decided to remain in the drawing-room and let Rainbarrow bring her in, but in the event there was a rather undignified scramble between us to get to the front door first as the Mini drew up.

One has become so accustomed to the frank look, the brilliant smile and the outstretched hand in the greeting of one's own countrywomen that anything else is rather chilling. I had been vaguely thinking about the *kowtow*, the bowing from the waist with clasped hands held vertically at nose-level, and should have enthusiastically responded in like manner but she neither looked directly at me nor smiled and she held out a limp little hand as cool and insubstantial as a dead goldfish. I like a good strong handclasp. However . . .

Paco drove the car round to the yard and the strange trio that was Rainbarrow, Juniper and myself, went into the house and Juniper said that she understood that I wanted her help professionally and she would be glad to give me her services. She spoke English perfectly but with not so much an accent as a strange intonation. Her voice was high but not loud. Not long ago I read somewhere that some woman's voice was 'like a Ming vase, wired for sound', and thought the description rather far-fetched, but it exactly describes Juniper's voice.

We went upstairs, leaving Rainbarrow in the hall below breathing heavily and watching us with the frustrated look of a stranded whale. As I followed her upstairs I admired her heels, the Achilles tendon as fragile as a violin string – how did they support her in the miles of trudging she must have to do round the wards of a London teaching hospital?

It seemed years since I had found the body of the girl and it was lying in the same position as I had left it, but further sunken into mortality. Side by side we stood looking down at her for a good few seconds.

'What a pity!' Juniper said at last and as I slipped off my jacket she went across the room and, picking up a towel, she tied it round herself sarong-wise. I felt ashamed that I was not as detached about her as she was about me and as I watched her return to the bedside I caught myself thinking of Robin's expression when he saw an extremely attractive female: 'Very, very dishy!'

We examined the corpse and discussed our findings as we washed in turn in the handbasin. I told her Rainbarrow had threatened me with a revolver and about the devilish silver cupboard. I told her that I thought him a madman and that I had appeared to agree to accept the money with which he had bribed me on condition that another doctor examine the corpse and sign the death certificate with me. I explained that this had seemed, at the time, the best thing to do but that now I appeared only to have sunk further into an extremely dangerous situation. I told her about Nell Fitton, friend of the dead Molly, whom I was sure he had shot a short time ago and I said that, now that it was too late, I believed I had dragged Juniper into something which I would have given a lot to have saved her from. I also asked if my wife had been at the station and it appeared that she had not but, as I had thought might happen, she had sent the local car-hire people to meet Juniper. The driver had spoken to her but, as Paco had already attached himself to her, the driver was sent away without explanation. My wife would be entirely bewildered, not to say worried frantic.

'Now,' I said as I put on my coat, 'what are we going to do?'

'Next I must tidy her up,' she murmured and set to work without the slightest suggestion that I might help. I took off my coat again and helped her to straighten the limbs which were now stiffening quite quickly; she had not intended a reproach but I felt ashamed that I had not thought of it myself. I had never laid out a body; to me a body is simply a complicated piece of junk, I never waste time over them, but Juniper's attitude showed a civilized respect and compassion. Finally she arranged the girl's hair becomingly round her waxy face and drew the sheet over it and, as she walked round the bed to smooth the sheet on the other side, her foot came in contact with something which she pulled out from beneath the valance: the instrument. As she held it up for me to see there was an impatient banging on the door.

'Time's up, you two!'

'It wasn't there before,' I declared firmly, 'I searched the room. The Spanish woman must have planted it. I remember her leaving us suddenly.'

'It is a crude and nasty thing!' and as she spoke Rainbarrow burst impatiently into the room. He saw the instrument, as Juniper held it, but the expression on his face did not change at all.

'Well? Well?'

'My colleague and I are in agreement,' I said slowly. 'I shall have to inform the Coroner as soon as possible that a dead body is lying here, I'm afraid I have no option.'

'It was a miscarriage, that's what it was.'

I shook my head firmly. 'A meaningless assertion, taken neat, as it were! In this case the actual cause of death is obscure but it was an abortion which could not possibly have been self-induced.'

While I was speaking Juniper had put the instrument into the hand basin and unwrapped the towel that was round her. She now walked across to the bed and gently turned back the sheet from the face. Rainbarrow moved across the room and, after staring for a moment or two, he burst into loud childlike sobs, an unexpected reaction to say the least of it. He crouched on the edge of the bed and blubbered like a child with a badly grazed knee. I found it surprising, as he had already seen the body.

Juniper, close to me now, murmured: 'He's a poor old man.'

'He isn't,' I contradicted. 'But we can slip away now and I'll telephone the Coroner from home, if we're agreed about time of death.' We were.

I will say this for the old man; he seemed genuinely shocked and upset, so much so that he did not appear to notice, absorbed as he was in his own private sorrow (which, as I now know, was that of a child deprived of a promised treat) when we slipped from the room. We tore down the stairs, and I found I was pulling Juniper's hand as we went across the hall, through the green baize door and along the passage to the back door, where the old car stood – he had left it locked.

I might have known it, of course; the Mini wasn't there. The stable door stood wide open: the Mini gone.

So were the Spanish couple. They'd hopped it and it didn't seem to matter whether Rainbarrow had advised them to go or whether they had done it on their own . . . they'd gone. Seen from any angle it was the best possible thing they could have done. Bereft of my car, I stared helplessly round the deserted stable yard and suddenly the air was full of the fantastically loud telephone ringing; there was even a bell outside in the yard.

'Quick,' I snapped, 'answer it before he gets there, say you're the foreign maid and can you take a message.' I pulled her back along the stone passage, through the inevitable swing door and across the hall: 'There it is, on his desk!' and she picked up the receiver and cooed into it like anybody's foreign maid.

'No,' I heard her say, 'I am sorry but he cannot speak for the moment; he has asked me if you will leave a message . . . yes . . . yes . . . I am to tell him: *the policeman has died*. No, the *what*? Oh, yes . . . *the policeman has died*! I will do so.'

I was standing by her as she gently replaced the receiver. She did not turn and face me, as any other woman would have done, and only now have I become accustomed to her indirect Eastern methods. Always their eyes slide away from you, they lower their lids and their faces are expressionless. It takes a bit of getting used to but, once you get the hang of it, other people seem, in comparison, crude and obvious.

'I am to tell a person called Micky, *the policeman has died*? ... Does it mean what it seems?' I am bound to admit that her laugh was not a laugh but a slight hiss; if she were the villain and not the heroine of the day, I could let it get hold of me, call it sinister and say that it gave me the shivers. Actually it didn't do anything like that, that little hissing titter, it had the effect of making me feel that she and I were the only sane ones in a mad, mad world.

'It may be the telephone call to his nephew that he has been waiting for all day,' I told her. 'Come, let's run for it.' And I wondered if I were doing the wise thing as we dashed for the nearest door, which happened to be the front; we would be fine targets as we raced up the drive; he could pot at us for quite a few seconds from a first-floor window. We would have to keep to the wall of the house and make our way through the orchard out to the farmlands at the back, sheltering ourselves along the hedges wherever we could.

But the telephone bell had roused him from whatever state he may have been in; he stood at the top of the stairs and shouted at us as I tugged at the locked front door, then lumbered down and prevented our passing him by standing in front of the door to the kitchen premises. I simply waited, sick at heart, for him to bring out his pistol again but he didn't. His face had collapsed and, though his teeth were still bared in that awful rictus, it now appeared to be from mental pain.

He said: 'You surely don't imagine I'm going to let you go now, do you? I thought I had made it clear that the death certificate would have to be signed before you leave the house. Otherwise *I* shall leave the house and *you* will stay.'

The trouble was, I knew that was roughly what was

going to happen, I couldn't see any other way out. There was a curious pattern about the day; right from the start, this beautiful summer day, in itself totally unreal, with a blazing sun in a clear bright sky, had had a deliberately executed design about it. Miss Cloverley-ffane's day out, the early call, Robin's news, the body, the metamorphosed junk dealer, the Chinese girl, anything could happen now, absolutely anything.

In that unfortunately realistic 'mind's eye' of mine I could see the headlines telling of the deserted house with no less than four dead bodies (that was nothing, really, there are often five when a man murders his wife, three children and then shoots himself). And I have often noticed that the more bodies there are, the less general interest there is: the murderer is always some demented creature who denies everyone personal participation by killing himself, thus depriving society of a just retribution.

The local *furore* would be big but the national interest small, a general practitioner in a country town, a Chinese postgraduate, a couple of tarts . . . and an elderly man whom the police wished to interview and for whom a watch was being kept on the ports. Not even Front Page!

4.30 P.M.

And then, with that perfect timing for which the whole day was notable, the thing for which Rainbarrow had been waiting all day happened. Micky, around whom everyone else swung as planets round the sun, arrived – *not*, as I have since discovered should have been the case, in a large white car but in a small green van. *Not*, as planned, in a smart charcoal-grey pin-striped town suit with a white satin tie, but in a track suit. *Not* with his smooth manner I had seen upon that one occasion in my consulting-room, but with a sullen, angry expression on his face.

Not (sorry, I must go on with these negatives) holding a despatch case packed with fivers, and there was hanging from his pocket the nylon stocking which it seemed he had been wearing over his face. Finally, *not* with the smart white calf dressing-case he had intended to take to Spain but holding behind his back a small weapon which I could not see well enough to identify.

His uncle pushed us in front of him as he heard the van stop outside and, taking the huge key from his pocket, he turned it in the lock and we were able to have a good long look at Micky as he stood swaying slightly on the great doormat and stared from his uncle to us and back at his uncle.

The first thing I felt was surprise that he should be wearing a track suit.

'Got company?' he managed to say. He was not as big a chap as his uncle, who now gave up, put one hand on the younger man's arm.

'Molly's dead, Mick. She's lying up there *dead*, boy!'

'Christ! Today of all days!' He looked at the gun that the old man was holding. 'Oh, it's like that, is it?' Pause. 'Who the hell are these?' Evidently meaning Juniper and me. 'Oh, I know you . . .'

'You've met me once,' I said coldly.

'I've kept them here, Micky, she's a doctor too, and I've kept them here because, for all anyone knows, this Dr Lavenham may be a guilty man: there's nothing to prove he didn't do it and I must keep him here because the girl's lying dead up there and the doctor refuses to sign the certificate.'

'He does, does he?' But Micky had a great deal on his mind; he nibbled at the nails of one hand, and Juniper said, her high clear voice cutting into the deep, dark thoughts of uncle and nephew like a wire through a cheese: 'I have a telephone message for you . . .' Pause.

'It rang as I was upstairs by the death bed. Tell Micky . . .' Pause.

'I was to tell you . . . *the policeman has died* . . .'

It only needed that for him to go berserk with the suddenness that must have been familiar. He was like his uncle. He swore dreadfully and shouted oaths which were unintelligible cries of rage and as he brought the revolver from behind him to shoot, Juniper gave a piercing scream and fell to the ground, the neatest thing I've ever seen, perhaps one-sixteenth of a second before he actually fired . . . wide because his aim had been distracted. Incidentally, I'm not sure which of us he had intended to hit.

Don't get the idea that I have ever been any good at Rugby football but I was pretty hefty at school and enjoyed a term as full back simply for the skill with which I could fling myself at an opponent and bring him crashing down. No one liked me because, out of sheer exuberance, I tackled people right, left and centre for the pleasure of bringing them down, rather than in any sort of team spirit. I felt once again, and I hope for the last time ever, that elation as I brought him down, even though he fired again wildly twice and, as I sat on his head, I twisted the gun from his hand and, pointing it at him, I got up. From the floor he actually laughed up at me: 'Three – that's it!' he shouted. 'That's the lot.'

It didn't dawn on me what he meant until I opened the breech and found it empty. So two had, presumably, been used for the 'policeman'?

4.35 P.M.

It is easier to be a vet than a doctor because all the vet has to do is to diagnose the trouble; whereas a doctor has to determine the nature of the disease in spite of everything that the patient has to tell him about his symptoms. Thus the doctor has to make a rapid assessment of the character of the patient whom he has often never seen before and knows nothing at all about.

I know Lombroso, the Italian soothsayer, with his skull measurements of the female delinquent, and *the brigand has an enormous occipital fossa* and all that jabberwocky, is out, but there was a sound idea at the back of it all. I find myself occasionally thinking something like: *his eyes are so abnormally close together that I'm sure he's telling me a pack of lies*, so I disregard my own observation completely. A few minutes later, faced with another patient, I can also think: *he's giving me the long straight look that only an inveterate liar can give*. So I try, and up to a point succeed, in not being in the slightest degree influenced by appearances.

Micky was well built with a good strong crop of hair growing low down on his narrow forehead and down his cheeks in magnificent sideburns. He had the wide apart eyes common in the Irish countryside and, though I did not see it often, a charming smile (which I remembered only from his visit to my consulting-room); he was the prototype of every girl's super-conman of the 'sixties. He didn't have to be nice, kind, amusing or clever, all he had to do was to affect every female within sight. He had no incentive to be what I would call decent, for want of a better word.

It was a problem how to cope with him and I felt so ill-equipped for it that the more pressing problem was how to get away from him. There was a pretty chaotic scene in the hall after Juniper's timely collapse. One of the shots had gone right through the ceiling and the second had ricocheted off something and the third through an old oil painting into the middle of a Scottish loch, leaving the Highland cattle drinking apparently undisturbed.

Congratulating Juniper, I picked her up and Micky dragged himself together and there was a lot of staccato, half-heard talk while I, my bag snatched up in one hand and with Juniper's tiny hand in the other, tried to push past Rainbarrow and nephew to the front door and the small van standing outside, but there wasn't a hope. We were hustled into the drawing-room, the door was shut, and Juniper was saying, with her little hissing laugh: 'Surely they're not going to keep us here?'

'It's absurd, isn't it?' I agreed. I laughed a little too, but it was a nervous laugh rather than an amused one. 'I promise you nothing like this has ever happened to me before. Progress has brought its own problems but some of them are awfully like some of the old ones, aren't they?'

'They've locked the door!' she exclaimed in astonishment.

'There's been a smash and grab of some sort in or near London; I'm sure he's got the jewels or money or whatever with him; they're probably counting it out now and they'll offer a large share of it to us, provided we don't talk. It seems clear to me that Micky is the boy-friend of the dead girl upstairs and she was the one who was going to take out the loot tonight via a night flight to Gibraltar. Perfectly simple except that she chose the wrong time to have an abortion (it seems absolutely mad to me, however...) and he's shot a policeman, not so mad because it is a thing which is very apt to happen if you're armed. Anyway, this is no place for us,' and I went across to one of the long sash windows, undid the catch and tried to heave it up but it didn't move. I then noticed the small round cavity of the special key used for that particular burglar prevention device on sash windows to prevent them opening.

Irritated by my lack of success, I picked up the first thing that came to my notice, a large garishly-coloured Satsuma vase and hurled it at the pane. The sturdy Victorian glass withstood it and shattered the vase, pieces of which flew all over the place. There was a hideously ugly Japanese ewer made of bronze with a carved dragon curled round it; though it was absurdly heavy for its size I snatched it up and threw it as hard as I could. It was a perfectly splendid sensation and relieved my feelings more than somewhat as it went through the plate glass with an appropriate crash. After all the noise it made the hole made in the bottom pane was enormous and I was having a go at the remaining jagged edge with the brass curb when they both came back into the drawing-room and Micky and his uncle fell upon me; Juniper retreated to the fireplace, taking refuge, I happened to notice, beside the only other female in the room, the marble caryatid.

I was outnumbered, outwitted, out of countenance and distinctly dishevelled; more in sorrow than in anger they stood back and watched me straighten my tie, push back my hair and generally tidy up.

For all the tumult and the shouting it seemed there was only one answer: a cup of tea. Presently we were all seated round the kitchen table, the males of the party in various stages of nervous exhaustion drinking supposedly reparative tea.

Between loud noisy sips Rainbarrow gave expression to the reflective mood in which he now apparently found himself, with his gun beside him on the table.

Was it then empty?

'So our country doctor is going to try to get out by force, is he? It's a pity you did that, Doctor. You've smashed a window I won't ever be able to replace for sheer sturdy quality and you've shown yourself to be a bloody fool, if you'll excuse me. We can't let you go, we can't afford it.'

'You mean, you can't do anything so ridiculous as keep us prisoners here . . .'

'Well, we've got to face it, son – ' he addressed his nephew – 'if these two won't see sense we've got to make them, and how to make them?'

'With guns, I'd say!' Micky was eating thick slices of bread and honey to restore his morale and he spoke through it.

'Tut tut, boy!'

'It's you've always said guns do the trick!'

'Have I indeed! That's very, very interesting.'

'Of course you have!'

'I've got one of the best collections of pistols in the country,' Rainbarrow boasted to us, 'it's my hobby. It started with clocks, then I had to sell them because I needed the money. So I took to guns and I've got a good collection locked away in a cupboard in my study. They all work! When my sainted sister, dead now, God rest her soul, sent her boy over from Ireland to take up his abode with me, she never expected he'd go off his rocker about them. Unbalanced, that's our Micky! Like a lot of young people nowadays, from all accounts.'

'Come off it, Uncle,' Irritably, Micky stuck his crumby

knife into the honey jar.

Rainbarrow leaned across the table and shook a stubby finger: 'But I've told you over and over again ... the gun on its own will talk, I've said. You don't have to fire it and if it's not loaded you can't fire it ...'

'I told you so ...' Micky jeered in a high-pitched mimicking way. 'What sort of nut goes about with a gun that's not loaded?' He pulled his cup nearer to him and sat with elbows on either side of it, hands distorting his face into a grimace. 'Dear God! Whatever made Molly be persuaded now?' He glared at me broodingly. He repeated: '*Now*. If you'd only done what I asked, Doctor, she'd have been alive now. You're responsible for this!'

'It was completely impossible for me to do what you wanted, you must know that,' I said. 'You seem to think that because you want a thing it must naturally happen. Well, you're wrong if you think any doctor would do a casual abortion, for whatever amount of money.'

'Wicked lies!' Micky shouted, banging the table. 'Isn't it, Doc?' And when I didn't reply he gave me a filthy look and told me that it was all my fault; in common humanity, he said, *I* ought to have done it. Common humanity, he repeated, pleased with the phrase.

I remarked that I had said all I had to say on the subject.

'You smug brute!' he shouted and other things, and I glanced at Juniper in a look of apology.

'Dr Lavenham is a very respectable person,' Rainbarrow said bitterly, 'very well known and well-liked in the district; it was a great mistake ever to get him in on it. Respectability,' he practically spat, 'he'll die of it!'

'I wanted Molly properly looked after,' Micky said, his voice thickening with tears, 'I went to the best I knew of... it was no room at the inn ...' He only just succeeded in not crying but his self-control added fuel to his resentment.

Rainbarrow said something rather weird and out of character. 'Don't weep now, Micky son, it's no time for tears,' he said. 'You're going to have years and years for that. It's this beggar we've got to think about now.' He meant me. 'Quite aside from Molly, if we let him out he'd go straight to the police about you.'

'Okay!' Micky gave me one of his long, straight looks. 'You may as well know the lot. My uncle and I run quite a profitable business between us. He does the plotting and I do the rest. We're greedy, he and I. We want the best for ourselves. His idea of the good life is to live in a great castle of a house, eating marvellous food and drinking good wine, messing about with his guns, riding his tricycle into the town where he's known as a Dear Old Gentleman. And my idea of the good life – ' he paused and once again his voice thickened as he swallowed the tears of self-pity – 'is the luxury block of flats in Torremolinos, the girl and the deep blue sea!' He put his head down on his arms to hide the expression on his face.

'So?' I said at last.

'So . . . every so often . . .' He left it at that but I wanted to know more.

'You plan a smash and grab.'

'That's a stale old expression. What's a handful of rings nowadays, anyway?'

'What was it then? You must forgive me if I'm out of touch.'

'Betting shop. A split new one in the East End; it's owned by a boyo from my home town. His dad has had one back home for years, and his father before him.'

'You mean – ' I know I sounded a real old square by the

jeering smile that passed across his face as I spoke – 'there was a stick-up this morning and you got involved with the police? And one was shot dead.'

'That sort of thing.' The sarcastic expression still altering his face. 'We'd got it all marvellously worked out, we always do, but in this case there was a pal of mine behind the counter as manager. And when I say pal I don't mean just anybody; I've known this bloke for years; he's got a shocking record, how he ever came to be taken on there beats me; and they're supposed to be fussy who they employ! But taken on he was, by pure blarney. Most firms like to get their money into the bank by three o'clock on Friday when they close, but this boyo from back home doesn't trust the banks nowadays, and quite right too, there isn't one you can't break open if you really want to take the trouble.' He took a great gulp of tea, it was clearly a relief to tell me, he liked talking about it. 'Mark you, I could've followed the boss back home with the money bags, tonight. I could've. But that's not me, I don't like beating up folk. I hate violence.'

We sat round and deliberated this information silently.

'So what do I do? I go in, I walk right through the folk standing around the door, waiting for the first results and making up their minds whether to pop in and make another bit or not to, I go in and there's a stick-up, as you call it. And my pal the manager who's had it all wrapped up ready, so to speak, hands it over and out I skip, see?' After a pause: 'Banks don't open Saturday now, but never mind banks, the manager chap in charge had taken his bite, OK.' He was talking and talking, half boasting, half confessing.

'Wearing the stocking over your face?'

Surprised, he looked at the stocking still emerging

slightly from his pocket and thrust it back out of sight, like a child found with an unsuitable toy. He irritably denied this.

"Course not, what do you take me for? My pal behind the counter isn't exactly a swift mover at any time and by the time he'd got over the shock and shouted for help I'm in the green van and away. Do you see?"

I was staggered into exclaiming: 'It can't be as easy as that!'

'It isn't . . . it isn't. You've got to have the nerve! And you've got to choose. I drove off pretty smart and that was that . . . or should have been. I reckoned I'd be safe when I'd gone a few miles through the suburbs and got myself out on the way to Romford marshes. You've got to know where to go. I hired this little van for the day, and parked me own car out there at a garage that's pretty well off the beaten track. Said I'd be coming back for it in an hour or so, and changed my clothes. Well, I was back in an hour or so but someone at the garage must have had an idea about me . . .' He broke off to wonder how on earth that could possibly have happened.

'Well, son?' Rainbarrow prompted him impatiently.

'The cops was waiting, they was *bloody* waiting for me at the garage . . .'

Rainbarrow jumped up from the table and paced angrily about the kitchen, ignoring the birdcage which he passed several times without a look. 'You should never have fired, boy. How often have I told you . . . you should have shown the gun but never, never have been the first to fire it.'

'You've never said don't fire, Uncle. You never said it.'

I believed that completely.

He went on talking, relieved to get it off his chest, excited . . .

'But as a matter of fact I did remember what you've often told me. I drove up unsuspecting, see, and there was this garage attendant and another and they was watching me come and it was like they were nudging one another and I thought: Hallo! what's up and I saw this greengrocer's van parked and I kind of got on to it in a flash; straight on from there leads nowhere much, they could have run me into the marshes that way; I had to turn; I got into reverse quick enough . . . took them by surprise . . . And then this joker stood in front of me with his bloody arms wide apart, like he was stopping me, right in my path. Of course I put out my hand, with the gun in it, and still he didn't move, so I fired it, to scare him; he jumped a bit but it didn't move him, so I let him have it, twice. I aimed at his legs like you do.'

'You blasted young fool!' Rainbarrow thumped the table surface violently.

'But only his legs, *only his legs* . . .'

'You didn't take aim, you just fired regardless . . . ah, dear Christ! You'll get a lifer for this and it'll *be* for life . . .'

'Not on your life . . . Unk.' It was a very feeble joke, but brave-ish.

5.00 P.M.

From time to time we glanced at Juniper; I wanted to catch her eye to give her a reassuring wink, which I felt very far from feeling but she sat with lowered eyes and an absolutely expressionless face, like one of those smooth Chinese images.

'Well, what do you think about it, eh?' Rainbarrow asked me, and then, and as I write it now it all seems as though I were recounting a bad dream, he said something like: 'They made traitors dig their own graves before they shot them in the back, but we're going to let you off the donkey work.'

'And leave us in the silver safe?'

'Thank you,' Juniper murmured musically.

'Let's stop this comic opera talk,' I suggested. 'You're impressing nobody but yourselves. I want to get back to my wife; she'll be desperately worried.'

'Is it likely, Doctor? I ask you seriously, is it likely?' Rainbarrow peered at me over the top of his glasses.

I was staring across the table at Juniper, willing her to look up.

'If we let you go, Micky here'll get a lifer and I'll get seven years for receiving, because that's what I do, receive. You've accepted what I offered for keeping quiet about Molly, but I can see now you only did that to gain time, didn't you? Eh, didn't you?' He thrust his beastly face close to mine and I did not bother to answer.

'So I'm not even going to waste my breath asking you to accept part of what Micky brought down today in exchange for . . . going on your way without a word to anybody. You're far too respectable for that, and as I've just said . . . you'll die of it.'

There was a long pause and from the absolute stillness of both of them I really believe that they hoped I was going to accept their bribe and leave it at that. I'm one of those who believe that we still have a splendidly efficient police force. What it seemed essential to do at the moment was to get away before they got themselves worked up into actually killing us both.

'You'll certainly die of the anxiety of disposing of two bodies,' I murmured cosily, 'in your state of health . . . with your blood pressure! And that would give Micky three bodies to dispose of.'

Four if Nell Fitton were shot dead. I glanced at Rainbarrow, but his manner told me nothing.

I pushed my chair back from the table and crossed my legs elegantly, Bulldog Drummond to the life except for my ill-cut trousers and clumping shoes. 'An awful lot of digging, you will agree. And all that heavy work wasted when the police start examining the ground, inch by inch, searching for three missing persons, or four or even five.'

'Oh, very smart; but if I die of a stroke – ' he choked a little over the word, he didn't like saying it because he thought it all too possible – 'Micky doesn't have to bury me along with you two. I can have a good sound death certificate and a decent burial with plenty of nice flowers.'

'Ah, yes!' I agreed, 'and as you would be dead, Micky could put the blame of Molly's death on you and go off to Spain with a light heart.' But as I spoke I was hardly thinking of what I was saying, overshadowed as I was by the sickening possibility that the mysterious disappearance of Dr Lavenham could not be connected in the slightest degree with the house of Rainbarrow. I went over the day so far, in my mind, and there didn't seem the least thing, other than some extremely abnormal coincidence, that could connect me with Rainbarrow or Rainbarrow with me. Nothing at all.

'This day began very badly for you, Rainbarrow,' I said solemnly. 'You have this early-morning shock and you have been in a state of extreme tension all day; you cooked a rich meal and ate it very quickly, you also ate much too much, your blood pressure must be so high that if I took it now the sphygmomanometer would blow up.'

'Why didn't you tell me that at the time you took my blood pressure, Doctor?'

'I oughtn't to be telling you now; knowing it is bad for you. But I must admit I don't care much if you do drop dead now, even though you are my patient. It's worry that pulls the trigger . . .'

'Aw, stow it . . .' Micky cried impatiently.

'So it's silly to kill two people for the sake of a life that's nearly over anyway.'

'You mean . . . mine?' he snapped.

Surprisingly Juniper moved; she put her little hand on his sleeve (and I now saw for the first time that she was wearing a pretty sapphire engagement ring) and he looked at her sharply. 'Mr Rainbarrow,' she said in her tinkling voice: 'it may not be as bad as that.' He looked at her sharply.

'I have known people with very high blood pressure who have lived for years.'

Now what was she up to? I watched the effect on Rainbarrow, that hater of women doctors, with amusement. Through narrowed eyes he looked at her with extreme suspicion.

'My own father has high blood pressure. He is an old man but he leads a busy life. He knows how to live,' she said impressively.

'*I* know how to live,' Rainbarrow boasted.

She shook her head slowly, her beautiful creamy eyelids lowered: 'No, I do not mean how to live your life, I mean how to keep alive. My grandfather lived to the age of one hundred and nine and he only died because he allowed himself to do so. He only died,' she murmured, 'when he wished to do so,' and in the ensuing silence her voice seemed to die away with metallic vibrations such as are left in the air when a bell stops ringing.

5.20 P.M.

But Micky was impatient, he couldn't care less about his uncle's blood pressure, so I judged it the right moment to put things in perspective. I said: 'I can't believe that two successful people such as you and your uncle can delude themselves about the exact situation. There's no problem. Look, this is the way it is: it is my duty to report the death of the girl Molly. Right? It was unfortunate that she should have chosen to have this illegal operation performed just before she should be taking your stolen cash out of the country. Right? But that need never come out. I can report the death to the Coroner and tell him that in my opinion the illegal operation was performed by a woman employee who, I have every reason to believe, and I hope to God it's true, is returning to Spain.

'I can also report that while I was on my rounds this morning my car was stolen, I could lie so far as to say it was stolen from the market place. Right?

'I need not mention to anyone what has happened here today, and I am sure that if you let Dr Ah Mee and myself go now, driving us as far as the main road in your van, we can keep our mouths shut. This is quite unethical because everybody has a duty to help the police, but I also happen to have a duty to look after my future daughter-in-law and I am prepared to keep quiet about you bloody couple of crooks in order to save her any further . . . any further risk.'

I waited for some immediate response.

There was none.

Sharpening my tongue, I went on: 'If you detain us here any longer you are complicating things for yourselves immeasurably. We can't stay here alive for long, that's obvious, and for us to stay here dead would make it more difficult than ever for you. In planning the sort of thug function you've carried out today, everything should be simple.' (I addressed Micky.) 'As it is, it is so complicated that it's bound to fail. It has failed, even you should see that, with a dead policeman to account for.'

'It was simple,' he shouted.

'It was sweetly simple,' the uncle concurred, shaking his head.

'Well, there's one thing obvious, which makes the whole affair far from simple: the police are on your track. Otherwise why should they be waiting at the garage on the marshes for you to come?'

I sat back and folded my arms because what I had said seemed absolutely irrefutable.

'They wasn't waiting for me!'

'You said they were!'

'Not for me personally.'

'You mean, it's the sort of garage frequented by bandits who park their limousines there while they perform their plunderage and return there later to pick them up?'

He rubbed his face agitatedly. 'Not at all, not at all,' he said, 'I was looking the perfect gentleman when I arrived. I changed there into this gear, not exactly running kit; I do quite a bit of cross-country running all round here when I'm around, you might have seen me, and what could be more likely than I should want to do it out there, along pathways across the marshes? And what more likely than I shouldn't want to take my car along those muddy lanes?'

'Micky's got a silver trophy or two, upstairs in his room, for cross-country running,' the uncle said complacently.

'That's the way we've always worked, made our plans to tie up with something we'd do every day, always making a good reason for being where we are at the time of the job; something we'd be doing anyway...'

'Well,' I remarked, 'I'm absolutely fascinated with this glimpse into the underworld.'

He gave a snort: 'Underworld! There's a lot of people live by their wits what don't class themselves underworld, believe you me.'

I said: 'We all live by our wits but when it comes to murder, some of us jib at that... and some... don't... and the ones who don't... I'd call them the "underworld" for want of a better name. They belong to the nasty underbelly of society we don't often see down here in the country. But to return to the garage on the marshes. However much of a gentleman you may have thought you looked, there must have been someone who thought you a crook, a gentleman crook, of course...'

'They was waiting for someone else!' he shouted.

'Don't kid yourself, Micky, they were waiting for you. They've kept your car and they've got the clothes you left in it when you changed into what you're wearing now.'

'You don't think I'd leave a scrap of identification, do you? I've got two driving licences, two insurance certificates, three names, three addresses... and I don't leave any of them in the car, ever. I've got two sets of number plates, and just for luck, two lots of trade plates, and I take them with me wherever I go; they're in the hold-all I brought along, and so was the gun until I took it out. They'll trace the owner of the number plates on the car to a chap who's been out of the country for the past three weeks; a sales representative with a bachelor flat in the

West End. And they can search the flat till they're blue in the face, they won't find one scrap of anything that will connect it with me at all. Nothing at all. And there's nothing to connect me in London either with this place or with Torremolinos.'

'I can see you have to work as hard as anyone who earns their money legitimately. I wonder you find it worth while. You must be as fully occupied as any businessman, making all these elaborate plans and evading Income Tax on top of it all,' I said.

'I've got to do some careful thinking, you bet!'

'The police do some careful thinking too . . .'

He pushed back his chair impatiently. 'It's taken me four years to build up my business and it's cost a lot of money, the upkeep . . . I'm not letting it go without a good fight to keep it, I can promise you that. If Molly hadn't been so scared of going off to Spain for a few weeks in her condition everything would have been all right. The total loss would have been one car. It's you being here that mucked up everything. *You* . . .'

He swung his arms impatiently: 'Come on, Uncle, don't let's mess about any longer. Let's get to the gun cupboard . . .'

'Don't be a fool, Mick, those two can't be left alone; they've done enough damage as it is.'

'For God's sake let us go!' I shouted very loudly, startling myself as much as I shocked everyone else. 'I've been here much too long as it is, let us go . . . it doesn't need me to report you both; the police will catch up with you anyway. I don't have to tell them where to come, they'll come all right . . .' I really was yelling.

I wonder, now, if they were on the point of letting us go. It was fairly obvious that the two wished to be alone together, they didn't want us with them any more than we wanted to be there. There was a pause, a silence broken only by the faint twittering of the love-birds, but no, it wasn't quite quiet. We were in the kitchen, remember, and from the kitchen one moved out into the service corridor, something which one finds only in old-fashioned houses. The passage from the green baize swing door to the back door had several doors opening out of it, the coal hole, the larder, the pantry and . . . and the silver cupboard.

I could hear a faint and seemingly far-away shouting. I hadn't really forgotten Nell Fitton, though she seemed an acquaintance of years and years back, but I had long since numbered her among the dear departed. When you have an average of twenty to thirty patients die a year you get accustomed to the idea of death, you don't brood over it, you can't. You think . . . they're dead and what a pity but that's that. And that was how I felt about Nell Fitton and I was as shocked as though she had actually risen from the dead when I heard her faint screams answering my shouting.

5.45 P.M.

I threw up my head like a nervous horse and a kind of tremor shook Rainbarrow. Micky was sitting in as lounging a position as was possible in a kitchen chair, his two feet propped in front of him on the edge of the table; he was glaring sullenly at them as though they were two enemies. I am sure he had heard nothing, he was too absorbed in his own woes. Thinking it over now, I think that Rainbarrow didn't dare to tell his nephew about Nell Fitton; it would be just one more thing to add to his troubles. I also guessed that if Nell Fitton had not been occupying it, Juniper and I would have been in that silver safe, leaving uncle and nephew to pursue their plans. As it was we were badly redundant, though they couldn't bring themselves to let us go.

I now know that Juniper, too, had heard Nell Fitton's cries but at the time she gave no sign of it. She looked across at Micky and asked in her clear silvery tones who it was who had telephoned the news: the policeman is dead. He could not have been more shocked if she had struck him across the face.

I took it up: 'Yes, who was it? You've just told us nobody connects you with this place but how did they come to telephone here?'

For a few moments he looked young and unprotected from the icy winds. There was, then, somebody who connected him with his uncle Rainbarrow at his country mansion. Someone other than Nell Fitton.

'It was a woman who phoned, it was a woman's voice,

wasn't it?' I said.

She did not reply.

He sat forward and tried to catch Juniper's eyes by staring up into her face.

'It was not a young woman,' she murmured.

'—!'

'The manager of the betting shop? He was in this with you,' I suggested.

'No. Of course not!'

'How do you know?'

'He hasn't the slightest idea where I live, either in London or here. We meet at certain pubs. He's never seen me at home and he doesn't know anything about this place. He got his rake-off for this job three days ago!'

'Well, clearly somebody does,' I remarked lugubriously and added some advice: 'I'd clear off, away from here as soon as possible. Upstairs there's a ticket to Spain by a night flight after midnight tonight; there's a name on the passport; I'd be on that plane if I were you. Of course,' I went on thoughtfully, 'it's in the name of Miss Molly O'Dare and nobody's likely to mistake you for her. Still, with the identities you've got and a spare passport or two, you can always use one of them and buy yourself a ticket. That is, if there's a seat going at this time of year.'

The old kitchen clock hanging on the wall had a comfortably cosy note as it ticked away the minutes. I don't have to try to relax, I do it naturally, otherwise I would have died of a coronary from acute tension a long time ago. But it was clear that both uncle and nephew were in a state of very sharp stress indeed and that must have been pretty much the way Juniper was thinking too, for she said: 'You will have to relax, both of you, or your uncle will die and you will give yourself away because of the condition of your nerves. One becomes clumsy, stupid and careless when one is tense and nervous.'

Was it the sound of her voice? Her stillness? Or what was it that did, in fact, seem to engender a temporary feeling of calmness and security? I felt it and I am sure the other two felt it. Micky continually ran his hand across the lower part of his face but he sat more slumped in his chair and his eyes were quieter.

Rainbarrow was as attracted to her as a pin is to a magnet. He leaned across the table, she moved to sit down opposite to him and for the first time I saw her giving a direct look instead of the sliding-away glance.

'How do you relax?' Rainbarrow wanted to know.

'We accept.'

'Come again?'

'We accept.'

'Now look . . .'

'Not only as doctors but I think as a nation, we Chinese learn to accept. As doctors we *have* to learn to accept. We are good doctors, you know. In China we were doing acupuncture thousands of years ago; it often works when Western medicine has failed. But when both the old methods and the new fail . . . we have to admit that there is no medicine for Fate.'

'Doctors have to have sympathy,' the old man argued, fascinated, 'and that's not sympathetic . . . "no medicine for Fate"; what comfort is that?'

'No, we Chinese are not sympathetic,' she agreed, 'we laugh when we see an old man fall . . .' She went across to the birdcage and opened it.

'Don't do that!' he shouted, but she put a finger inside and drew it out with both love-birds sitting on it. She held them to her cheek, then walked back to the table and sat down, the perching love-birds on her finger between them.

'At home I take my love-birds for a walk...'

'Well, you're not taking them for a walk here,' he grumbled, but he was clearly enchanted.

'... we walk in the evening, when it is warm, along the Street of a Thousand Grandsons.'

'And what about your old dad? Does he walk too?'

'Sometimes...'

'Is he overweight, like me? I take exercise though, nearly every day; I use a tricycle.'

'Ah, yes?'

'He walks, does he?'

'A little sometimes, but when he is not at his business he is usually playing chess.'

'Playing *chess*?'

'Yes.'

Rainbarrow rubbed his chin. 'How rum!'

'That way he learns patience,' she said. 'My father has calm fortitude and passive patience, thus he is prepared for the troubles that may come his way. He does not wear himself out with anger and rage.' She timed the pause nicely and added, at exactly the right moment: 'Like you.'

'Yes,' he agreed, 'I do wear myself out, that's just what I do!'

'Tranquillity comes from within,' she murmured, 'not from coloured pills in a bottle...'

I could see the way things were going and I felt a calm elation. She would look after the old man and I could tackle Micky alone. I said loudly that I wished to visit the lavatory. Rainbarrow was too absorbed, sitting across the table from Juniper with the love-birds between them, to take any notice of my request. Micky shot me a dirty look, then reluctantly pulled himself to his feet and shuffled out with me. It was as easy as that. He waited immediately outside the hall cloakroom (which had, by the way, a small barred window), facing the door so that there was no chance of my springing suddenly out at him. His hands were in his pockets, though, when I came out, so he didn't expect an immediate attack.

'By the way,' I remarked casually as we started to return to the kitchen, 'how long is he going to keep that girl shut up in there?'

'What girl shut up in where?'

I could hardly believe that he hadn't told Micky . . .

'It's only that I am afraid she might be short of food and water.'

'What bloody girl?' he interrupted rudely.

'Why,' I exclaimed, surprised, 'Nell Fitton, of course; Molly's best friend.'

Again he swore my least-favourite oath. He went on to name the Holy Family, one by one, and to ask me in outraged tone of voice what she was doing down here 'today of every blessed day in the calendar?'

With the pleasure of someone bearing important and rather bad news, I told him that she had come apparently by train this morning, because she was worried about her friend Molly. Mysterious as the events of the day might appear to anyone else, Nell Fitton found no mystery about it. She appeared to know that Micky was going to carry out a robbery and that Molly was going to come down by train and wait quietly at the country *rendezvous* till he came, and that later that night she was going to be driven to London Airport by Micky, taking a night flight to Spain with whatever it was Micky had stolen, when it had been shared out with his old uncle. She knew that Micky would follow the next day. And last, and most important of all, she knew that Molly was pregnant and scared to death of spending the next few weeks in Spain with the baby growing inside her and the chances of having it removed growing less and less with every hour that passed.

A real friend, Nell Fitton, I declared. Knowing of her predicament, she had sent to her home in Ireland for Molly's mother, and in the meantime Molly had run away by taxi, train and again taxi, from the flat in which they both lived. Nell Fitton had come after her in her own car to help her friend . . . only to find that she was already dead.

As I spoke, Micky's face was not turned in my direction, he was looking straight ahead and I was speaking into his typical ear, not completely cauliflower but getting on that way, something that one would not notice in the ordinary way but I had syringed out far too many ears not to pay attention to the one into which I was now pouring a flood of bad and not altogether correct news.

'These damn girls and their flats,' he swore.

'You've just told us that not a single soul knows of your connection with this place and within five minutes I've been able to show you were wrong . . .'

But he was hardly listening.

'All they ever think about is men, and when it's not their own boy-friend it's the other girls' . . .'

'Yes, yes! But about the particular two who are your business: at present one is dead and the other probably slowly dying from lack of oxygen in the silver safe.'

He begged me to keep my trap shut while he changed his clothes. Thus I was compelled to enter his room and while he changed into black corduroy slacks and a black polo-necked jersey, on this hot summer's afternoon, I examined his silver running cups, of which he had about half a dozen and a couple of medals. He rolled up his plimsolls in what he had been wearing and stood in front of me, irresolute, with the bundle between us.

'I could have burned this if it had been last year when Uncle had a coke boiler but now with this new oil-fired central heating I don't know what the hell to do with it.'

'Leave it on the railway line,' I shot off carelessly, 'where you leave other unwanted objects.'

He gave me a long, long look, hard-breathing. 'You're tired of life . . . you want to die . . . it's people like you make people like me have to help you off. You stick your necks out so far you're screaming for it. I don't want to kill you, but you bloody well shout for it. I didn't want to shoot that nark. But he asked for it, same as you . . . throwing out his arms like he was crying: "Shoot me, for Pete's sake, fire!"' He touched his gun to draw my attention to it. He took up a comb and ran it through his hair. Somehow, as he combed his hair I found him more vulnerable.

'Have you viewed the body?' I asked in his own vernacular. He went on looking at himself in the glass as though he had not heard. I repeated the question and he snapped back that he had heard the first time; he was not deaf.

'You know, I think you should,' I said in friendly and familiar tones. 'You toss off the fact of death so lightly. "Kill you", you remark, "help you off" . . . you talk as though you had, or were about to, trample on a black beetle. I don't think you've ever stopped to think . . . what is death? You see a beetle, you stamp on it . . . it's a dead beetle. But with people it's not quite the same. Come and look at the body of the girl you loved,' I urged in fine cinema-prose.

I waited. He was still looking at himself in the mirror on his dressing chest; it was a little too low so he had to bend his knees to see himself.

'No, thanks.'
'I think you should.'
'What the hell do I care what you think?'
'You should, you know. Your fate is in my hands!' I thought that was the kind of corny cliché he would understand and, sure enough, he did.

'You mean *your* fate is in *my* hands...' he said but with a certain lack of enthusiasm which made me wonder if he had lost his taste for killing, and if so, for how long?

6.15 P.M.

I turned back the sheet and exposed her face and neck and bare arms as waxy-white and opaque as an artificial water-lily, her closed eyes now further sunken into what looked like bruised sockets; dark Irish eyes she must have had, the sort that didn't need mascara; big and childlike and pretty fatal. I thought I saw signs of the rigor mortis round the face. I went across to the window and looked out at the only summer day this summer which, because of its rarity, seemed lovely beyond one's dreams. And I hadn't been out in it at all, not even to have a quick spring round my roses.

Like somehow slipping towards coma, I felt my wife and my home, my garden, my dog and even Miss Cloverley-ffane were becoming less real, something remembered, something that was quite a long time ago.

He was silent for so long that I had to turn round. He was standing beside the bed, looking down at her and I realized that he was probably thinking, for the first time in his life.

'She isn't there, is she?'

'No,' I agreed, 'she isn't.'

'It's . . .' Rather pathetically he gesticulated with his raw hands, groping for words, which he eventually found: 'It's just one of those things.'

'Yes,' I agreed again. And because we couldn't go on staring down at her indefinitely I pulled the sheet up and asked conversationally what he was going to do about her; was he going to take her body down to the railway line after dark, so that it would be dealt with by train after train? 'Like,' I added dangerously, 'the other two about which your uncle unwisely informed me. He told me to frighten me.'

He neither started back, nor swore, nor glared; we might have been having the most amicable conversation over a couple of bottles of Coke and two hamburgers, instead of standing with the body between us and double murders in the air.

'That was Uncle, not me,' he vouchsafed, 'I really hope Uncle's not going nutty. He's been a receiver in a big way for a long time now and it would be a pity to go and muck everything up just when he's about to pack it in.'

'Pack it in?'

'Retire. It was these two chaps came late one night and got to quarrelling between themselves over the share-out. It's always over the share-out people break up. One of them got out his gun and shot the other; they was blind drunk, Uncle said. It was easiest for Uncle to shoot the one that was left and that's what the old boy did. It was all tidied up here by the time I got back, the trouble was far enough away from the house for Uncle to deny that he heard a sound or had ever seen either of the chaps who were killed. He said he didn't even use a gun, he just made them punch drunk and sent them off in their car.'

I cleared my throat politely because I wasn't sure if my voice was working properly. It came out fairly all right but not a lot of it: 'You mean, he dragged them back into their car and drove it to the level crossing?' Rainbarrow had made a point of saying he couldn't drive, I remembered, hence the tricycle.

' 'S right.'

It would have been a relief to have gone dizzy, as men are reported to go at a particularly ghastly sight, but I stood there immobile and took it. These two men who had been in their small Mini van were taken to our hospital, piecemeal, after a particularly long goods train had hacked them to bits in the early hours of one morning. They were small-time bookies and it was said by Rainbarrow at the inquests (and corroborated by various friends and relatives) that they had been to the Races and called at Rainbarrow's for a meal on the way home. Not much money was found on them.

Rainbarrow had described the meal and the drink they had all had and no one was in any doubt that it was an evening spent in excessive conviviality that had caused them to be half-way across the level crossing, with the gates open to let them pass, when they were hit by the goods train at well past midnight. There had not been any doubt about it in my mind until this morning when Rainbarrow had drawn a gun upon me. Such is one's sense of security.

There is a delightful machine on Bristol station which calls itself a reviver of tired feet. You stand on it and put your penny in and it oscillates beneath the soles of your feet so that the whole body vibrates. I was reminded of this now, as I stood beside the death-bed, and vibrated slightly hoping it did not show.

'That is the man,' I managed through clenched teeth, 'who strongly advises you never actually to fire.'

'That's old Uncle, always shooting off his top but not a bad old chap, really.'

I waited for the shock to subside a little before picking up the handbag from the dressing-table and taking out the air ticket. I held it out to him: 'Why not use this? I oughtn't to say it but I think you should go, and go quickly. If you've really shot a policeman you may have hit the headlines by tomorrow morning and it will be too late. You've got the ticket, all you have to do is to say at the airport your girl-friend couldn't come and can you use her ticket, she'll be coming later, on another ticket; they'll let you through all right. You can get away with a lot at two a.m. As far as this girl goes, you haven't committed a crime; most likely it was the Spanish woman Encarnita something and she'll be out of the country, we hope, by now. Your uncle will have to take some responsibility but as Encarnita was an employee, he is not legally involved. And as far as the other crimes go . . . maybe the Spanish sun will burn it out of you. Tomorrow morning when I stare in horror at the photograph of you in my *Express*, I will telephone the police and tell them all I know!'

'You will? And then Uncle will go down in flames . . .'

'He'll do that anyway, but in the meantime he may have to go to Broadmoor because his behaviour, you must agree, is not rational. For his own protection, he should have a spell at that place. He won't find the food up to the standard to which he is accustomed but they're kind and understanding.'

He flung away from the bed and walked over to the window where I had been standing. 'Nevertheless,' he said with his back to me, 'I'm not taking any risks, I'm keeping you and your Chinese girl-friend here till Domesday, if possible.'

I put the air ticket back where I found it.

'Of course. By the way, what about money?'

'There should be around two thousand quid in cash in the hold-all. Uncle has to have half of that. But there's enough to keep me going for a bit. I've just about paid off for the building of the block of flats. There's enough to live on from the rents and I was hoping to settle down there.'

'To marry?'

'I never said nothing about marriage though I might

have gone that way, in time.'

'A pity she didn't know. I dare say she thought you'd throw her away when you found she'd still got to have the baby.'

'She did, did she?' And his face took on that pugnacious look which, I realized, it had lost for a time. For a short while he had been a fairly reasonable human being but now he suddenly remembered that he wasn't.

6.30 P.M.

At a time like this, things people say in the course of conversation certainly stick in the mind. I remembered Rainbarrow asking Nell Fitton what she thought she was gaining by staying here and Nell irrelevantly replying that if she was turned out of the house she would go back home and tell Molly's mother everything. I thought: poor ineffectual creature, wandering into a criminal set-up on the humble mission of going after her flat-mate who was in trouble! Since Rainbarrow shot with the unimpeded readiness of a fruit farmer shooting bullfinches, I really wondered why he had only pretended to shoot her. To scare the Spaniards? He had certainly done that, but it couldn't have been the first time the Spaniards had been scared. Had they assisted with the drunken bookies? Had that been the first occasion they had heard real shooting? Had he bribed them to keep quiet about it? Or had they, quite simply, been off for a day and night?

Finally I wondered why, finding myself in what I could only call a 'den' of robbers and murderers, of abortionists and bandits, I should be in the slightest influenced by what anyone said? The trouble was that in trying to assess the truth, I really didn't have anything else to go on. Dear old Bulldog Drummond was sometimes alone on the scene of the crime; he could sniff round for clues, tangible ones. I had no clues at all, it was all guesswork: is what he/she says true ... or not? And I hadn't had enough time myself to think things out. Also, the only time I had been alone, since the plot had thickened, was in the drawing-room when I had found the safe behind the ravished caryatid.

'So as I see it,' I went on, 'two people that *I*, even I, know of, know you're down here. They are: Nell Fitton and whoever it was who telephoned. If you've got a police record . . . you have, haven't you?'

'They've never caught me yet,' he said, but in his new subdued mood he merely stated it without boasting.

'They have your photograph in their album, though, I bet. They'd get that from informers. And when they're going the rounds after any big robbery, they pay a call on you. Now don't deny that . . .'

'They don't often find me in and they don't know me under my own name and they *don't* know I come here. Uncle has been a receiver for over thirty years, he's no amateur at keeping things secret. Years ago, when he had that junk shop in the town, he was one of the biggest receivers in the country. Since he moved out of town and became a country gentleman he's only dealt with the big stuff and not often, at that. You don't think an old hand like Uncle would take on a nitwit, do you? He's trained me. I've told you I've two other identities; it's only here and in Spain I'm meself.'

'Your overheads must be quite something. You're three people, two of them paying rent, probably not Income Tax, but rates, attending the doctor, having cars, charge accounts, girl-friends . . . jobs . . . it makes my head ache to think of it. It's much easier to be a perfectly respectable, hard-working executive.'

'It's not that complicated, it's pretty simple really. One of me has a service bachelor flat in . . . let's say a big block of flatlets in the West Central area. That's the salesman; I come and I go and nobody takes a spot of notice.'

'And the second of you?'

'The second of me has a small junk shop on the edge of Portobello market. I'm only open Saturdays and Sunday mornings: all the rest of the week I'm touring the country in a pick-up, picking up.'

'It's Saturday today. How come you're not there?'

'I'm in Dublin this weekend. I sent a postcard to a young chap I know who's at the London School of Economics; met him in a pub a year ago and found out he could do with a bit of a job at the weekend to give him a spot of extra cash; he's got a dooplicate key and he's let himself into the shop early this Saturday and looks after things. Often I'm there with him but if I'm not . . . I send him a p.c. Do you see? When you think things out, it's not all that expensive. It's a matter of thinking things out.'

'Where does the second of you sleep, if you do sleep?'

'The me with the stall in Portobello market sleeps in a boarding-house in North Kensington, when I'm there. They've known me ever since I came over from Ireland that first time under another name.'

'You go back to Ireland a lot, do you?'

'That's another thing . . . you might say there's four of me, I've another aunt on Dad's side there and I'm often over . . . like this week when I sent off the postcard.'

'You're hard to get, Micky.'

'I'm hard to get all right.'

'In fact, if it weren't for sex, you'd be impossible to get.'

'How do you mean?'

'I mean, it's the women who are your weak spot, isn't it?'

'I reckon it's a lot of people's.'

'But you've kidded yourself you're making things doubly sure for yourself by getting Molly O'Dare to do your carting for you.'

'Kidded myself? You're wrong there. The customs is on the look-out for chaps like me, specially one making a habit of going through Gibraltar. "What's he up to?" they ask each other after they've seen you a few times. And then one time they ask you to kindly step along and strip to the buff. Not that they'd find anything that way on *me*; but they'd only have to open my baggage and the bundles of fivers would fall out all over their bench.'

'Whereas they would never dream of asking a lovely creature like Molly to open her case?'

'If they did . . . she'd be able to take their minds off their object.' He gave a twisted sort of smile. 'It's . . . they get to know you, that's the trouble.'

'Molly's only done it twice for you?'

He nodded.

'And this was probably the last time?'

'Definitely!'

'I begin to see . . .' I said slowly. 'Poor girl.'

'She got a damn good holiday thrown in,' he retorted defensively.

'I'm sure. I wasn't thinking of that. I was thinking about the others.'

'The others?'

'The girls before her.'

He swung restless about the room. 'Oh, come off it! You're making such a thing of it. It's only the last eighteen months . . . since the block of flats has been building . . . I've been planning security for meself; once I've got everything straight out there, there'll be no need to keep on. It's only just for now . . .' he almost whined.

I squared up to him. 'You've been very frank with me, Micky,' I declared, 'and thanks. It helps me to get things straight in my mind. I understand perfectly now why she chose to do anything so silly as have an illegal operation just as she was about to start off on her trip to Gibraltar with a bag of stolen notes. She was dead scared you were going to ... brush her off like you did the others. You've been trying, unsuccessfully, to get the pregnancy terminated; you tried me and ... was it that something good in you stopped you sending her any old where? That's what probably made her have that little bit of extra love and faith in you that she wouldn't otherwise have had. She thought that *she* might be the one you at last really loved. And it was for *your* sake that she allowed that damned Spanish woman, if it *was* she, to have a go. She wanted to greet you with the splendid news that the baby was all over and done with when you joined her in Torremolinos. There is a name for chaps like you but, God! it's corny. I won't insult myself by using it.'

'All right, all right, calm down, Doc. As a matter of fact I did carry on about the ... about it. I did a bit. I mean ... if she'd waited to tell me till all this lark was over ... I'd enough on my mind. It's like ... I mean ... you know how it is, Doc ...'

'You're trying to say that when you're planning and carrying out a dangerous and complicated robbery your sexual appetite is sharpened.' I have observed embarrassment equal to that of a middle-aged Victorian spinster in sexual gluttons of his class when discussing their troubles.

He was shocked by the crudity of what I said, and reddened to the roots of his hair. 'That's just about it,' he mumbled. 'We never decided how far on she was but it's my guess she started off being sick right from go. If she wasn't actually being sick, she felt sick and she looked sick, too. I was never really rough with her, I swear it, Doc. That day I came to you, I came because I wanted the thing done proper, by a decent medical man. I know there's a big risk when you go to one of those dirty old dames there are around. But I thought ... well, never mind. She took it into her own hands, and look what's happened! And to think it happened right under Uncle's nose! I could laugh, I could really, if it was a laughing matter.'

I swung away towards the window again, irresistibly attracted by the weather I was being denied.

There are a number of young men in our town who look like Micky; they are house-painters and builders and lorry-drivers and labourers; a few look like thugs and thieves but they aren't bad at all, once you get used to them. Micky looked slightly more refined and was the first rip-roaring criminal of his age and vintage that I had talked to for any length of time. Oddly enough, I hadn't a doubt in my mind that everything he had told me was true.

I stared out wistfully, thinking what an isolated house it was, how there was very little hope of the laundry arriving, late on Saturday afternoon, or even the parcel post. The next visitor to the house would be either the Sunday newspaper boy tomorrow morning or the postman on Monday morning and I had reached the maudlin stage of wondering what would have happened to us by then. I saw the top of a train and a moment or two later a black dot appeared where the drive rose to its highest point and then sloped down to the railway. A black dot that became a familiar sight, a policeman's helmet: Sergeant Greef very slowly pushing his bicycle. When he was in full view, having reached the top of the slope, he mounted and came towards the house at a good freewheeling speed. Sergeant Greef and his assistant Constable Payne, everybody called them Grief and Pain, were in charge of a small hamlet a mile or so down the main road where there was a chicken-packing factory, a public house and a group of council houses. One of us in turn attended a surgery there every other day and we knew Grief and Pain very well indeed.

But unfortunately Micky had come across to the window to stand a foot or so away from me and was blowing his nose. Over the top of his grubby handkerchief he saw Grief describing a graceful curve in front of the house and dismounting.

'Jesus wept!' and with the pious exclamation on his lips, he grasped my hands together, pulling them behind my back in an inhuman vice-like grip.

The hired green van from the garage outside London was standing by the front door, surely every policeman in England would be on the look-out for it by now? Micky dragged me back towards the death-bed, pulled the sash-like belt out of Molly's Thai-silk dressing-gown that lay across a chair and bound my hands firmly. Then he let go of me and moved away to a chair beside the door, sat down, crossed his legs and lighted a cigarette which he took from an apparently gold cigarette case in the pocket of his trousers and lighted with an apparently gold lighter.

He put the gun within easy reach.

'We've been in this room long enough, you've seen all you need to see and more. Let's go!' I suggested.

'Relax, Doc,' he murmured, 'and we'll let Himself look after this. Uncle's good pals of the police; they've probably come to remind him he's to get a new TV licence. Saturday afternoon is the sort of time they would choose.'

He stared at me with a straight level look beneath his dark, threatening brows. He was master of himself again, he was tense and alert with excitement.

'It's no use measuring me up, Doc, I'm in training and fighting fit; you'd have no chance, no chance at all.'

6.50 P.M.

The account of what happened next is Juniper's. In the drawing-room now with the love-birds on the small table between them she was describing the details of her grandfather's diet when the front-door bell rang. She could tell that Rainbarrow was extremely startled but he made some attempt to hide it. He pushed the birds hurriedly back into their cage and taking her by the hand he went out to the front door; he told her to stand by him, where he could see her and just before he opened the door he whispered that he didn't want to hurt a hair of her head but if she made a movement or a sound of any kind he would be obliged to hurt her a great deal.

He opened the door about one foot, leaving it on the chain and apologizing like one keeping a tiresome dog inside. He did not invite the sergeant in, excusing himself by saying he was 'rather busy', and the sergeant, with the face of one about to report bad news, said he had called about the Spanish couple; he read out their names from his notebook, and said he believed they had been with Mr Rainbarrow as servants for the past eight months.

Rainbarrow's whole attitude relaxed when he knew the sergeant's mission and he said, quite affably, that they had, in fact, been with him for that length of time and today they had left. They had not settled down well and they were anxious to return to their own country.

The sergeant asked what time they left, then said that they had been involved in an accident on the main road, which must have occurred within a few minutes of leaving.

The man had been taken unconscious to hospital and the woman, he regretted to report, was dead; she had died an hour after being admitted to hospital, from multiple injuries. The car, he said, a white Mini Cooper with a black roof, was a total wreck. They believed, he went on, that the car was a stolen one and the man had probably not had experience of driving that particular make of car; he had taken Shepherd's Bend, Mr Rainbarrow would know that dangerous corner well, at much too great a speed, the car had left the road, somersaulted according to a witness and crashed into a tree.

Then Rainbarrow said that he much regretted to hear what had happened but he was by no means surprised. Though he hadn't been going to say anything, he now had to admit that the couple had been shockingly dishonest. He believed that they had stolen cars before; the man was fascinated by them and he had reason to suspect that they had on one occasion taken a car to drive up to London on their day out.

Sergeant Greef clicked his tongue and said was that so, and Rainbarrow said he had only recently come to suspect it and he had, in fact, given them notice as soon as he realized what a bad lot they were. He gave the impression, Juniper said, of a dear old man, unsuspicious and slow to blame, but reluctantly obliged to part with this couple of dishonest people when he found out just how dishonest they were.

The sergeant was prepared to settle down to a long talk but this was not so easy when he was kept standing on the threshold talking with the door barely open. He took off his helmet and scratched his head and as he replaced it he said he had a good idea whom the crashed car belonged to; in his opinion . . . and it was now being confirmed with the licensing people but being Saturday afternoon things were held up a bit, people being off out on a nice day like this ... in his opinion there wasn't a doubt about it that the car belonged to Dr Lavenham. The car had contained, as well as the foreigners' hand-luggage, a locked doctor's bag.

Mr Rainbarrow exclaimed that he didn't say.

Sergeant Greef solemnly reiterated his suspicions. Dr Lavenham's car was very well known for miles round, he said. The doctor drove like a bat out of hell. Furthermore he would jump out of his parked car and leave it without locking the engine or the doors ... 'he's always that hurried,' he added and also that nobody in the district in their right mind would steal it; it was quite understandable that a foreigner might pick on it, being as how he wouldn't know it was Dr Lavenham's car.

'How ... m ... soever,' Juniper copied exactly Greef's delightful Gloucestershire elongation of the adverb as being a sign of the length of his deliberation. He had telephoned to Dr Lavenham's house and Mrs Lavenham didn't know where the doctor was, been away since early morning, she had said.

That was Juniper's moment. 'He's here,' she piped, 'and he's being kept here against his will ...'

'One moment, one moment, Sergeant ...' Rainbarrow dragged Juniper across the hall into the study on the other side of the house, pushed her inside, slammed the door and locked it.

Later I asked Greef what had happened and incredibly he answered: 'At the time I didn't give it a thought, sir. I was writing in my notebook.'

When I protested, saying: '*What*! Didn't you hear the girl calling?' he looked confused and said he wasn't exactly paying attention, he'd a lot on his mind at that particular moment, and he thought it was some kind of kid shouting something. After shutting the child up, Mr Rainbarrow had come out of the front door, closing it behind him, and strolling across the drive with Greef, discussing the matter of identification of the Spanish woman's body, seeing him off on his bicycle, dismissing the interruption as the idiotic cries of his poor little niece from Ireland, a cretinous creature and almost out of her mind, he regretted to have to say. He dared say that the old man was looking after her while his unfortunate old sister was in hospital.

'Look, it's like this, sir,' Greef protested in his apologia later on to me, 'Mr Rainbarrow was a well-thought-of old chap, a bit queer in the top storey, and a real old character. It never entered my head there was anything wrong!'

'Evidently!'

But only last week when I had to syringe out Greef's ears I guessed at the truth: he's going deaf.

7.00 P.M.

'I'm sick of the bloody lot of you!' Micky shouted like a spoilt child, when we were back in the kitchen while another pot of tea was being made. 'Jesus! It's as public as a fun fair. What's gone wrong? Uncle, have you gone out of your mind?'

'It's the day,' he croaked, 'never in all my born days...'

'Day! It's a nightmare!'

'It's worse than you think, boy, it's a lot worse than you think.'

His nerve seemed really to have gone, events had bent him and the smile on his still red but now verging on purple face was clearly a wince of mental pain.

Micky's self-confidence was wearing thin, too. It wasn't one thing that had occurred to thwart him, he shouted, but everything.

Rainbarrow shook his head slowly. 'No, son, it's one thing. Just one thing. That child you caused to be conceived was ill-gotten; though it didn't live to call you Daddy it lived long enough to destroy you and me and all our works.'

They grovelled in their mutual Irish despair while I tried to catch Juniper's sliding-away eyes. It wouldn't be long now, it couldn't be long before we were rescued. It seemed to me it was just a question of keeping ourselves alive till help came. The spent Luger lay on the table beside the love-birds' cage. Not far away there was apparently a cupboardful of guns but it is not so easy to shoot straight with what the trade calls an antique weapon.

'Since I've not been able to have more than a word or two with my uncle in private since I got back, as everything has to be discussed like it was in a shop window because we've got company, I may as well say what I have in mind.'

He looked round at the three of us, challengingly: 'Molly isn't my business; her death has nothing to do with me!' Rainbarrow tried to protest but he was shouted down.

'Seems to me you've all got a good let-out with this Encarnita getting herself killed. There's nothing more for you to worry about, Uncle. The Doc here can ring up his bloomin' Coroner and tell him there's a corpse here and there's been foul play and the woman who done it's got killed in a car accident . . .'

'In my car . . .' I put in.

'. . . which they stole while you was here talking it over . . .'

'. . . for three-quarters of one day?'

'And the Spanish husband is still alive,' Juniper murmured,' when he comes round he can deny everything. He could say he was sent away with his wife because the doctor wished to do an illegal operation.'

'Just how fanciful can you get?' he mocked.

'He can say anything that suits him when he comes round. It's just one man's word against another,' I suggested. 'And there is one thing that doesn't fit, Micky,' I went on, 'and that is: who rang up to tell you about the detective you shot? Um? It's my guess you haven't an idea.'

Micky sat down at the table. He scraped up handfuls of his hair and pulled it. 'There is this girl-friend of Molly's who could have made a hash of this for me . . . she might have done it deliberate. She'd have been pleased I killed the dick. It could have been her telephoned but you say it wasn't a woman.' He raised his head and looked blearily at Juniper, who returned that she had said it was not a young woman's voice. 'Women! There's no end to their spite once they get it in for a chap.' He changed from pulling his hair to biting his nails and I changed from thinking about Nell Fitton as a pathetic, loyal, loving girl-friend and began to wonder if I myself were rather a stupid, bumbling old GP thinking I knew a lot about people and, in fact, knowing very little indeed.

'Tell us more about the girl-friend,' I suggested and as I listened to Micky I stared boldly across the table at Rainbarrow.

'Oh, she'd lots of girl-friends who could've . . . who could've . . .'

'Could have what?'

'Been the one that telephoned.'

I strained my listening powers to the utmost in the ensuing silence but I no longer heard any sound from the silver safe.

'How often have I told you, Micky?' the old man moaned, 'don't shoot first, I've said, and I've said don't ever let anyone else know your plans.'

'Don't I know it? I never did . . . I never have . . . I swear, Uncle, Molly knew nothing, only she was to come and wait for me here, today that was. And, by the by, why did she come yesterday?' He stared at his uncle, whose hoary head was bowed, as well it might be.

He went on: 'She was to come here today and wait for me and I was to take her to the airport tonight and she was to go off to Gibraltar by night flight . . . Oh! what's the point of going into it all over again!'

'There's a lot of point,' I said, 'talking it over reminds you of things, and I've been reminded of one or two things that have been said . . .'

'What things?' he snapped.

'Clues, that's all . . . clues!'

He dismissed me as the poor patient donkey and shouted rudely at his uncle: 'Why did she come here earlier than was arranged? Tell me that!'

Rainbarrow gave an elaborate shrug: 'As it turned out, to talk over her predicament with Encarnita, ask her to do the operation.'

'Rubbish! Rubbish! She didn't know the woman all that well, she'd only met her once before.' There was a long pause while the expressions on Micky's face changed with fascinating mobility as first one thought and then another crossed his mind.

Round about now I began to feel that if the opportunity to leave the place had presented itself I would have refused to go; I seemed, up to now, to have been flitting about on the surface of things and only now to be peering through cracks in the crust.

Micky banged his fist into the palm of his other hand: 'It must have been one of her girl-friends who telephoned; it couldn't possibly have been anyone else.'

Juniper murmured again: 'It was not the voice of a young woman,' and Rainbarrow raised his head and met my questioning glance.

He knew it could not have been Nell Fitton.

I knew it too. Because she was only a few yards away from us.

Why did neither of us say so?

7.15 P.M.

Somehow or other Juniper and I were part of the family, as it were. They weren't going to trust us alone for a second; they had to have us within sight; things had now become too desperate for them to worry about what we were going to do later on. *Now* was what mattered, and Juniper and I could have thoroughly messed up *now* for them if we had wished. Killing us wouldn't help *now*.

But Juniper and me-and-my-bag would have to prevent a happy ending for Rainbarrow and Micky. That seemed to me to be far more important than getting away. My wife, Miss Cloverley-ffane, Robin, my Labrador ... I am sorry to say I no longer gave them much thought; I was committed, as they say in the weeklies, up to the neck and well beyond it, to the top of my head, because I had begun to think to some effect. It was a ludicrous understatement to tell myself: things are not what they seem! It had taken me an unfortunately long time to realize it.

Whatever they intended to do we had to sabotage, and quickly, because the car was found and identified, and now it was only a matter of time before we were found. If much more time was lost in conversation there would be nothing either of them could do but shoot to kill, in spite of all the pious warnings about not being the first to shoot that Rainbarrow dished out to his nephew.

I picked up the Luger casually and weighted it in my hand: 'The first thing you'd better do is to re-load this, isn't it?' I murmured. 'You don't seem to realize what the Spaniards' accident means to you: once they've traced my car's number plates . . . you'll have had it, chums, it if weren't a Saturday afternoon, the only nice one this year and everybody out enjoying themselves, except us, they'd have been here for me by now.'

It was part of the curious lethargy that had come over them that neither of them answered. They were now no longer partners, there was something between them, neither could any longer trust the other. I wondered if it was the right moment suddenly to confront Rainbarrow with the request to open the silver safe and let out Nell Fitton.

I had no plan as to when to do this but I think perhaps I was saving it until such time as we were actually at the point of his gun so that I could throw it out in the same way that Juniper had flung herself to the ground, just as the revolver went off. There is nothing like a shock for affecting even the best of aims. That must have been why I kept my information as a secret weapon of defence.

There was an absurd impasse; if either one or the other left the room to re-load the pistol it would mean leaving the other with two of us; perhaps that is why neither of them made a move but sat looking sulky, each apparently absorbed in his own thoughts, as well they might be.

Having drunk the tea, we were still in the kitchen, but Micky indicated that he was tired and we were led by them both at gun point to more comfortable seats in the drawing-room, now bright with the early evening sun.

I sat down on the chair next to Juniper, edging myself closer to her. She was sitting with her habitually lowered eyes, her hands folded in her lap as though at a tea-party of her elders, her face impassive and expressionless. Would

Robin get tired of her serenity and start wanting to throw things about? Or is serenity of that depth sort of catching? I rather thought it was; not that I felt myself serene but I felt a gladness that she was serene, a kind of security.

'How are you, darling?' I whispered.

She smiled and looked at me sideways. 'If you mean how much more can I stand, the answer is quite a lot. I am not tired out, or even a little tired. I am fascinated.'

'Not bewildered?'

'Yes, bewildered, too.'

'What will Robin have to say to me about this?'

'He will be glad that I should have got to know you better.'

'Better than simply . . . coming for the weekend?'

'Of course. You and I are learning much about one another.'

'You might have been killed, Juniper . . . you might still be.'

'It is in matters of life or death that people really get to know each other; not over bowls of rice.'

She amused me. Our little exchange took place with pauses, over a space of three minutes or so. Her hair hung again to shoulder length, black and shining, the ends curled outwards slightly. Now she put her handbag on the table.

'It is hot, don't you think so?' She brought big hairpins out and twisted her hair, with a few flicks of her tiny wrists, into a knot on top, which she secured with only three large tortoiseshell pins.

'More businesslike,' I suggested with approval.

'Cooler,' she answered.

Rainbarrow raised his great craggy head and stared at her. 'I'm sorry if I hurt you,' he said unexpectedly.

Juniper rubbed her wrists: 'You did hurt me a little.'
'I had to get you out of the way, do you see?'
'Of course.'
'You nearly destroyed me. I don't want to have to hurt you again.'
'No?'
'No. So try to keep from meddling, that's all, my dear.'
I didn't then know what they were talking about but when Micky had brought me downstairs and untied my hands Rainbarrow had announced the reason for Sergeant Greef's call.

'How can I do that? Dr Lavenham is to be one of my family, and I of his.'
'Is that so?'
She nodded. 'His son and I are to marry.'
'Is that so? Quite a family affair, then.'
She nodded again.
'You think a lot of families, don't you, my dear?'
Another nod.
'Family means a lot to me, too. That's why I'm so fond of my Micky here. My only sister's son and she dead this twelvemonth, God rest her soul.'

Juniper said nothing, the incongruity of the remark probably shocked her but she showed no sign.

Rainbarrow jerked his head in Micky's direction. 'He's the only family I've got. I'd do a lot for him. But the trouble is . . . you spend years teaching them and then suddenly they're off on their own with a lot more to it than ever you've taught them.' He again lowered his head and stared down at his clasped hands which hung between his knees in a familiar attitude. 'Yes, he's all the family I've got and so there's nothing I wouldn't stop at to save him from a life sentence, nothing. I'd shoot you both if it meant getting Micky away safely,' he added in a gentle, kind, thoughtful way. 'Isn't it time you took yourself off, Mick? I know you want to get yourself off in the dark but the hanging about is getting on my nerves.'

Micky switched on the television.

7.30 P.M.

'All the same, I'd give a lot for you not to be here at all.' Rainbarrow rubbed his face like a bather gaspingly emerging from the sea and went on to demolish my secret weapon in its entirety.

'Ever heard of a young woman called Nell Fitton?' he asked his nephew.

Of course Micky had heard of Nell Fitton: he looked wary as well as weary but said nothing.

'She's a hell-cat, that one, she's everything I mean when I say women should be abolished.'

Rainbarrow stood up heavily and creakingly, like an older man than he was; for the first time the day's events showed they had told on him. 'I've got her here in cold storage for you. I ought to have shot her but I didn't; I only fired to scare the lights out of those two spying Spaniards. I know what *they* were up to, all right. Blackmailing me for much fine gold!' He gave a harsh bark of laughter. 'So I gave them something to blackmail me about and lo! they packed their traps and took off before I had time to pay them what I owed them. Makes me laugh. Didn't stop to make sure I had shot the woman . . . couldn't see them for dust. Well, they've got what they deserved!'

'Nell Fitton's never given any trouble!'

'No? You surprise me. She's given plenty this time, all right!'

'What the hell?'

'You may well ask, Micky, you may well ask . . .'

'And so where is she?'

'She's in the lock-up, boy, she's in the lock-up. She may have died from lack of air!' His chuckle sounded distinctly mad and Micky mooched up and down the kitchen, hands in his pockets. 'If not, she could come in useful the same way Molly came in useful when required,' the uncle added slyly.

'What d'yer mean?'

'Taking out the cash, taking it out of the country tonight, as planned.'

'Nell Fitton!' he exclaimed as though someone had asked him to eat something very unpleasant.

'Why not?' Rainbarrow said. 'Hell-cats have their uses. She's not a bad-looker, though she's no Molly of course. You can run her to the airport tonight, as planned with Molly.'

'————'

'No need to swear, listen. She's got her passport with her and she can use Molly's ticket. You'll be at the airport to see her off on the plane, then you can take yourself off on the very next plane anywhere; working your way back to Spain in a day or so.'

'. . . but they'll be sifting the whole crowd of departures tonight, looking for me.'

'Don't flatter yourself that you're such a distinctive type; two o'clock in the morning and the officials at the airport are as glassy-eyed as walking corpses. You won't have a policeman that's too alert at that time of a summer's morning either, Sunday too. Dammit all, boy, you've got to take some risks some time . . . you can't always be spoon-fed!'

He rubbed his hands backwards and forwards against one another, making a dry sound which got badly on my nerves.

He went on: 'You can leave these two to me; the doctor and I have got on reasonably well all day; I like his Chinese daughter-in-law, we'll be fine. Come five o'clock tomorrow morning I can let them go with my blessing. They can telephone the police and talk to them till they're black in the face, there won't be a thing they can prove against me, not even the attempted abortion, that can all be put down to the dead Spaniard. And it doesn't even matter if the husband says she never done it . . . husbands don't know everything.'

We must all have looked thoughtful and pretty uncertain because he went on: 'Look, accusing folk isn't enough these days. The doctor here can say I did this, I did that, I'm a receiver and a murderer (which I'm not) and an abortionist (which I'm not) and even a transvestite (which I'm not) if he likes, nothing to stop him saying it . . .'

'Never short of words, are you, Uncle?' Micky observed sarcastically.

'There's nothing to prove I've got anything at all to do with you, Mick.'

'You *are* a murderer,' I put in quietly, 'I happen to know that,' thinking about the second bookie whom he shot to match the first one and disposed of on the railway line.

'Prove it,' he shouted, spitting like an over-acting Hamlet; 'prove it, *prove* it!' he yelled. 'Prove it to the satisfaction of any one of Her Majesty's judges, and remember,' he added, 'who you're talking about. Me! Me! A nice harmless old man, known hereabouts these last thirty or so years . . .'

'He'd talk the hind legs off a donkey,' Micky observed.

'That's exactly what I am doing. You're a lot of donkeys the whole lot of you . . . the police too . . . that Sergeant Greef . . .' He choked with laughter, the choke becoming more severe until he was gasping for breath.

Like a lot of patient mokes we sat and waited till he had recovered; at least, Juniper and I were sitting, Micky was still pacing restlessly up and down, up and down. The love-birds, in their cage on the table in front of us, were now huddled together for comfort, taking refuge in each other from the storm of words hurtling about them.

'Good grief!' he gargled convulsively, 'that policeman wouldn't believe his eyes . . . couldn't believe his ears, he only knows what he knows, and that is I'm one of the nicest – the *nicest* – people living round here, he never comes to the house but what he's asked in for a cherry brandy, I keep a bottle specially for him, so I must be nice.'

Juniper put a hand on his arm. 'Don't!' she begged. 'Don't! You really shouldn't get excited, you know. My grandfather never did, never, whatever happened.'

Rainbarrow changed into a lower gear. 'You're right, my dear! Well now, Mick. Time's flying . . .' He glanced at the clock.

'Did Greef get a cherry brandy today?' I asked. And as he didn't answer I said I had thought not, perhaps it might cause him to think before long that Rainbarrow wasn't so nice after all. He ignored me.

'Mick.' No answer.

'Mick . . .' He looked beseechingly at his nephew through piggy red eyes.

'Look, Uncle, you can't make the Fitton woman do what you want; if you've had her locked away in there for any length of time she's not going to be in the best of tempers, to put it mildly. What possible excuse did you have for shutting her in there?'

'Plenty of excuse, boy, you'd be surprised.'

'I would. Poor old Fitton is harmless enough.'

'That's all you know, my lad!'

'She'd never do it.' But he said it thoughtfully as though there were a remote possibility that she might, if pressed. 'Why does she have her passport with her?'

Rainbarrow chuckled.

'Let's get on with it, then, let her out and see what she says to your idea.'

He shook his head, slowly but firmly. 'Not yet, not yet. It won't do her any harm to cool off.'

'Cool off? How long has she been there, for the love of God?'

'It wasn't for the love of God,' he chuckled gleefully, 'for the love of the divvil, Micky, the divvil himself.'

'Let her out, anyway.'

'I said *not yet*!'

They were suddenly flaring out at each other, shouting and glaring at one another; the nephew wanted the girl out, the uncle was equally determined to keep her in but in the Irish manner the tempers died down as quickly as they had risen. It was probable that there was nothing the nephew could do about letting her out because the uncle would certainly take care of the sequence of numbers that would unlock the safe; which meant, I thought, that if the uncle had a stroke and died, which he well might, with emotions running so high, half the house would have to be blown away with gelignite before we could release wretched Nell Fitton. It was doubtful if there would be much Nell Fitton left, anyway, after we'd blasted a way through those tough Edwardian walls.

Micky ran a hand over his face over and over again. 'I could do with a drink!'

'What's wrong with you, boy? You know you never drink when there's a job to be done.'

'Well, I'm drinking now!' he snapped and we all had to go into the dining-room where the drinks were and be offered liberal half-tumblers of the excellent whisky I had had this morning, so many light years ago, Juniper refusing any at all. It was even more absurd when we all filed back into the study and Rainbarrow unlocked the oak cupboard, on the shelves of which, carefully arranged, beautifully polished and oiled, lay his collection of weapons.

He loved them, he liked the feel of them in his hand, he touched them unnecessarily, and once I saw him testing the silken feel of the steel against his lips, as though he were kissing it.

'So you like to leave your fingerprints all over your guns,' I murmured.

'Oh dear, Doctor, how unobservant you are!' Rainbarrow pulled Micky across to me and twisted his hands, palm upwards, for me to see what had been done to him. He showed me his own, too. I had never seen it before but I realized at once that they had both had the skin removed from their fingertips and replaced by skin from elsewhere on their bodies so that the actual tip of the fingers was smooth pink flesh without a line. I'm never squeamish but the sudden unpreparedness of it almost made me eject violently the whisky I had drunk.

'Better than gloves,' he observed with stretched lips, 'gloves are hot, you get clumsy . . . and if you wear light cotton ones you can't drive a car, not that I drive one now, but I did.' He paused. 'You're not such a good doctor as all that; you've examined me physically a number of times . . .'

'Once only . . .'

'I thought you might have noticed and I was ready with

my answer, but no.'

'There were a lot of other things I noticed . . .' I said darkly.

'Such as?'

'Your bundle of hiss,' I declared loudly. I had remarked how easily he was disturbed by physical references and had he been slimmer he would have become slightly haggard: as it was, his stretched mouth looked more a rictus of anxiety than I had yet seen it. 'Your islets of Langerhans, your unstriped muscle *and* your canal of Knud.' Juniper let out a tiny hissing breath of laughter. I was really trying to scare him as much as he had scared me; his marble eyes were clouded with unease. 'I can't understand why you should have bothered to have that revolting operation done on your fingertips; I thought Micky here was the one who did the dirty work.'

'I've handled some things, I can tell you,' he boasted. 'They've brought me jewels here worth a king's ransom before they were broken down. I'm one of the best silver experts in Europe, I'd like you to know. Even your expert burglar has got to come to me to get some sort of value for the things they steal . . . and there must be no time wasted.'

'So you had your hands mutilated . . . well well! As Montaigne says: "It's the peacock's feet that humble his pride!"'

But he had turned his back on me and was looking over his stock of weapons again. Micky must have seen Juniper and me exchanging an amused look because he indicated me with his empty glass, shoving it rudely under my nose and saying: 'Don't make the mistake of underestimating me uncle; I've seen him light matches with a pistol at twenty feet.'

'Go away with you!' I laughed, 'he's a nonentity! The

man hasn't any character, he's just an assortment of attitudes. I've had all day with him and I'm not impressed. All one can be definite about is that he has the common characteristic of all criminals.'

'What's that, eh?'

'A self-conceit so abnormally developed as to become a kind of moral cancer and an ability to act the dear old gent, such as I witnessed this morning by the death-bed of that girl upstairs.'

Rainbarrow made a guttural sort of clotted noise and swung round, pointing the re-loaded Luger full at me. 'I'd stop fooling about, Doctor, if I was you!'

He turned to Micky: 'You'd better have this, it's small.' He picked an elegant little gun from the shelves.

'It'll take up a lot less room than this big feller, especially if you're going to carry it around. Now listen, I'm going to get Nell Fitton out, for convenience. I'll keep her covered because she'll be in a state, and you keep these two covered, Micky. I don't trust them, at least I don't trust the Doctor, he doesn't seem to like me. Forward march, then . . .'

8.00 P.M.

It just wasn't their day; if it had been, if their habitual luck had held, I wouldn't be here to write all this down for the record. The ancients never came to any important decision or started any momentous action without looking into the star position. If these two had thought of inspecting the night sky with a view to their own fortune they would have found

> ... *malignant and ill-boding stars,*
> *Now thou art come unto a feast of death* ...

Thus it was no coincidence that, as we were marched towards the deadly silver safe (much dreaded by me because I am distinctly claustrophobic) the telephone rang, a loud insistent clamour just above our heads in the service corridor.

He had been waiting, tense and on edge all morning, for a telephone call, but that was before Micky arrived. Now he jumped violently and went a blotchy, patchy purple. 'Who the hell is that?' He and Micky stared at one another, shocked beyond thought. It went on ringing.

'It is best if I answer it,' Juniper suggested. 'I am a foreign girl; if I answer it everything will seem to be all right.'

'It'll be the police, about the Spaniards,' Micky averred. 'They like to bring news of a death in person, now they're letting you know how Paco is, is my guess.'

We stood still, all together in the narrow passage and

waited for the ringing to stop. It didn't.

'Go on, then, you answer it...' And Juniper pushed her way through the service door, across the hall and back to the study whilst we followed her and stood around, Micky and his uncle watching her as they might watch a grass snake, ready for any unusual move on her part. But there was nothing remarkable. She said yes and no, and yes and no, she was sorry Mr Rainbarrow was not available, she was sorry she knew nothing about his nephew. She had no idea. The voice was not actually audible but the sound of it could be heard vibrating through the earpiece, interminably, the sound waves going up and down, up and down, up, up, down.

Then at last she replaced the receiver and returned to us, as impassive and unchanged, as cool and tranquil as ever.

'It was Lady Lakeland,' she announced, 'Molly's mother. Someone has told her everything.'

'*Everything*. What do you mean by everything?'

'Someone telephoned to her at her home in Ireland yesterday and told her the whole story.'

'*What whole story?*' Rainbarrow snapped impatiently.

'About Molly and her criminal boy-friend.'

'But who... *who*?'

Juniper shook her head but said that it must have been someone who knew a lot. 'She has flown to London from Ireland and called at her daughter's flat; there was no one there. The woman is in agony of mind. She wants Micky caught but naturally not her daughter. That's why she rang here earlier to leave the message that the policeman was dead.'

There was a long, palpitating silence.

Rainbarrow stared across at his nephew: 'Well, you've done for us now, boy,' he said wonderingly.

Juniper went on: 'She guessed Molly would be here, waiting for him ... or else she knew for sure ... all she wants at the moment is to stop Molly helping Micky whom she calls that thieving wretch; she seems to know all about her daughter's lover. She thought that ringing through with the message about the policeman might make her daughter stop to think. She is half mad with worry and she thought I was the Spanish maid who would probably try to prevent Molly going. I just let her go on ... what was the good of stopping her? Poor woman.'

She paused again and darted short slanting glances at Micky. 'She has been at Scotland Yard for hours, since she found the flat empty. She's in a hotel now, all alone, and frantic. It was the result of what she told the police that caused them to catch you, as she puts it, *red-handed*, whatever that may mean.'

I knew the signs by now and it wasn't long before his organizing ability came to his rescue.

'We'll take Nell Fitton's car, boy,' he said, knocking his clenched fist into the palm of his other hand.

'And we'll shove these two in there alongside Nell Fitton, they'll have plenty of time for exchanging confidences,' he leered at us, but Juniper went forward and touched his arm.

'You don't mean that, it was unkind, cruel, and untrue.'

He ought to have clapped us into that unpleasant prison then and there and if I had been on my own he would certainly have done that; there wasn't any other answer because as long as we were there, standing, sitting, waiting to be freed, we were bound, in one way or another, to clog up the works.

Every moment that he spent staring fascinated at Juniper was a moment nearer his destruction, but I believe that I actually witnessed a hypnotic braking power so that the man couldn't free himself entirely; she had hampered him from the first moment she arrived. To me he seemed to have ceased to be entirely practical, as he had appeared to me during the morning when he briskly hurried about his house and prepared a meal.

He stared at Juniper's ivory hand upon his sleeve fixedly like a dog that is about to vomit. 'Out of my way,' he said, but he made no move to shake her off. Meanwhile Micky had taken out no less than three passports which had bulged inside his hip pocket and was looking at them each in turn. 'I'll take the lot,' he said, 'and we'll see. Your passport is in order, Uncle, so get it out, and we'll take our golf-clubs, nothing makes you so dopey-looking. Change into that thick tweed suit of yours and I'll do the same . . .' He made a move towards the door but returned. 'Come with me, Doc,' he said with a jerk of his head, 'I want a word or two with you.'

Clearly they had planned something of this kind before, and since the nephew's appearance today they had, somehow, an understanding as to their plans in an emergency.

8.15 P.M.

He put the small revolver carefully within easy reach and made me sit at the far end of his bedroom, away from the door. As I watched him I thought that he could have earned a substantial living as a male model; in string vest and underpants, and finally in his country gentleman's tweed suit he was some girls' ideal man, well-shaped, low-browed head, strong brown limbs and a style about the wearing of his clothes. I thought what a waste it was all going to be when he was slouching around in the uniform of Parkhurst, or Her Majesty's informal dress worn by residents of Wormwood Scrubs Prison.

I murmured something of the kind, always unwilling to come in out of the cold and once again he begged me not to try to be funny. He was beyond being fussy about shooting, he said; since he had for the first time broken his resolve never to shoot to kill.

He swore as he broke a shoelace on his suède shoes and while he was fiddling with a fresh lace he told me what he evidently wanted me to know. 'I don't understand Nell Fitton,' he said, 'I thought she was said to be "so fond" of Molly. I don't understand why she followed Molly, why she parked her car away out of the drive and pretended she had come by train, it's all beyond me. But I just want to warn you about her. She's a bit of a mystery, that one.'

'Oh, thanks.'

I must put it on record that I did not at that moment believe either that we were going to be shot or that we were going to be incarcerated with Nell Fitton in the safe.

I had been threatened off and on all day and it had come to nothing; to me Rainbarrow was at the moment not so very much more than the street urchin who rushes up with his cap pistol crying: 'Bang, you're dead!' Even knowing how he had treated those unfortunate bookies and left two corpses to be mutilated beyond recognition on the railway line didn't convince me that he was a reckless murderer.

But Micky was, or at least he had become so. I've always believed that once you have deliberately shot at someone and killed them, the second time comes much more easily.

A spasm of annoyance at my manner crossed his face but his desire to talk overrode it. 'It's women get Uncle down. Believe you me, women is Uncle's cross that he's never been able to bear. He don't know where he is women-wise and if you ask me, he never will. He's all at sea, and that's why he's always swearing and shouting about them. He's a mis... myso... what do you call it?'

'Misogynist.'

'That's right. In a way he loves women, and in a way he hates them. And I can't get to the bottom of why Nell Fitton came here. I don't know her hardly at all; she's a nurse, do you see? She has off-duty time all sorts of odd hours and when I'd call at the flat I'd never know whether she would be there or not, unless Molly happened to have told me beforehand. She never seemed to take much notice of me but I know, because Molly told me, she was kind to Molly. She was untidy, that kid, always left a muck of dirty dishes in the sink, never took her fair share of the housework. She'd never been brought up to do housework, see? Nell Fitton slaved after her, she even washed her clothes for her when Molly was stuck. She'd press her things, too. I used to ask Molly sometimes if she had a boy-friend of her own and Molly would always say not that she knew of. She's staff-nurse at the hospital and on her way to being a sister one day, her work is her life . . . that sort. She's scared the pants off Uncle . . . or something.'

'Or something. Tell me, what did Molly know about this day's work? Um?'

He tugged at the new shoelace, scarlet in the face. 'Look, Molly was the reliable sort; it was the *fiff* time she's done this job for me, taking the money out. She never asked no questions, she did what she was told. I said she only done it twice, but that was from here, what Uncle knew about.'

'She may not have asked questions but you may have told her what you'd planned.'

'Never,' he said.

But I knew he had; he was too pleased with the plan and too sure of himself not to have boasted to his girl-friend, too conceited.

'You're not clever enough, that's the trouble. You've let your uncle down, he's the clever one.'

'All right, all right, I got the point first time.' He stared at me. 'How much would you take to get the hell out of here and your Chinese doll with you?'

'Don't let's start that again; your uncle has tried me on that one,' and I remembered the bundle of fivers, still in my pocket. 'And don't waste your money; you're going to need it when you're caught, employing a better counsel than the State will allow you, perhaps, to prove your innocence.'

'We're not getting caught this time.'

'Yes, it is the very last time,' I agreed sympathetically but not for the reason he thought.

He sprang up and tugged his golf bag from the space between his wardrobe and the wall; irritably he took out certain clubs and tossed them on the bed; carefully considering the weight of the bag, he finally left himself with seven. He slung the bag round him, picked up his small grip and with his right hand holding the pistol, jerked me up and followed me out of the room.

8.25 P.M.

This time when we returned to the kitchen Juniper was sitting at the table as before but the birdcage was open and empty. Rainbarrow had transferred the birds to a small travelling cage with a handle and they sat close together on a tiny perch, very overcrowded, the female with her face hidden on her husband's breast, the male darting angry looks all round him and clucking his extreme disapproval.

'For God's sake!' Micky shouted, then swallowed his indignation and said mildly that he was ready, it was time for his uncle to dress the part. 'And step on it,' he urged, 'I've got to go and pick up Nell Fitton's car from the main road where she left it.'

'And we can't leave the van outside any longer ... go and lock it up in the stable, Mick. I'll look after these two, then I'll dress in a couple of ticks when you're back.'

He stood beside the table, the small birdcage in his hand, and looked down almost fondly at Juniper. 'The first time I've ever met a woman worth talking to! And I've got to leave her; isn't it too bad! If I could trust you and didn't think you'd scream out when you were going through the customs, like you did when Sergeant Greef was here, I'd take you with us; two golfing gentlemen with a young Chinese lady ... that would fox them.'

I felt like sitting down beside her and putting my arm protectively round her. I felt she was my Aladdin's lamp, my talisman, that somehow she was going to save me. I didn't think: *save us both*, I distinctly remember thinking:

save me; rather extraordinary, as though she was made of some special immortal substance that didn't need saving.

'Yes,' Juniper agreed with Rainbarrow, 'it is a pity you cannot have me with you; I would serve a good purpose, I would keep you from living your life foolishly so that you could continue to enjoy good health. Because if you do not die suddenly, you will soon have the disadvantages of old age about which nobody can do anything but yourself.'

Micky came back into the kitchen then, having locked up the van, briskly hurried his uncle upstairs to dress for the journey. In his absence he brewed the three of us some deadly strong tea, pouring it out with an unsteady hand and solicitously offering us milk and sugar before shovelling spoonfuls of sugar into his own cup and drinking noisily, saying he dearly preferred tea to anything stronger. Nobody said anything, I am sure that I was listening, listening for the sound of a police car's tyres on the drive.

Still Saturday and mid evening. The sun's rays were slanting now and edging their way through the kitchen window across the roofs of the yard buildings. It was now almost an effort to remember home; my wife would have telephoned to Robin, and Robin, in a minor panic, would probably be on his way down in his sports Sunbeam. I hoped he would drive carefully, not frantically. Miss Cloverley-ffane would have packed up her picnic basket; their day's trip would probably be over and she and her friend would possibly be looking for somewhere to have a light supper, or high tea. My Labrador would be wandering about, tail hanging limply, or else lying right across the entrance to the drive, a habit of his when he thought I had been away long enough.

I couldn't bear to think about my wife but I thought about the Clover; last year, on her summer's outing, she had worn a suit which she had inherited from a dead sister who had been a keen lady bowler; it was cream serge with square shoulders and a long pleated skirt; I was sure she would be wearing this suit and she would have had her hair done yesterday so that the grey curls would spring and bob about in the warm sun. Now that I might never see her again I discovered that I loved the Clover; I should never laugh at her or make fun of her again; I gritted my teeth when I remembered all she did for me and how little I did for her. I should never again call her Mrs Tiggywinkle in her grey musquash coat . . . but it was probably too late.

I gave myself indigestion drinking the thick orange-coloured tea and that made me feel tired and long for home. When there was a shout from Rainbarrow that he was now ready and to come out into the hall, we trooped, Juniper and I somewhat wearily, out yet again, Juniper carrying the small birdcage.

The luggage was on the hall table, two canvas grips and two golf bags; Rainbarrow's piglet of a hat was lying beside it but he was standing in front of the looking-glass wearing a deerstalker hat in which he looked laughably 'up from the shires'. In fact, I was caught unawares and laughed aloud; people in funny hats always make me laugh. Juniper nudged me reprovingly.

'Where did that damned woman leave her car?'

She had left it in the yard of the Badger, the pub in the village where Grief and Pain operated; she had had a drink there and caught the bus to the gates, so Rainbarrow now announced. She did not wish her car to be seen here.

Micky's mouth dropped open. 'How the hell am I going to get there?' he asked, bewildered.

Rainbarrow, still gazing fascinated at his own image, clicked his tongue and said they hadn't been thinking, had they? The only way of getting to the Fitton's car was in the van, which Micky could leave outside the police station. 'Take your trade plates off,' Rainbarrow giggled, 'and we'll see how long it takes them to find out where it comes from.'

'And where's the key of Nell Fitton's car?'

This did bring him up sharp. He toyed with his gun, turned it over and over in his hands.

'She was wearing a shoulder-bag,' I put in, 'and I didn't see her take it off the whole time. She'll have her bag in there with her, Rainbarrow, you'll have to let her out to get it.'

Every minute that we could delay them . . .

Micky was becoming more and more fidgety and impatient but Rainbarrow might have had all evening to get away; he didn't want to go and that was the truth; it seemed almost as though he were playing a delaying action.

'We can't very well go in the van,' Micky shouted, remembering. 'There's not enough petrol for one thing!'

'My poor boy, we can't start without petrol!'

Micky banged his fists against his forehead.

Give it up, I thought; give yourselves up; everything is against you, you'll never make it!

8.45 P.M.

It must be difficult for anyone who has not been held at the wrong end of a loaded gun for a long time to imagine just how imbecile and inept one feels under the circumstances. At the time of what was called the A6 murder, when a mentally deranged young man sprang out of nowhere and held up a young couple (who were making love in a car parked in a stubble field late one evening) at the point of a revolver, I remember thinking as I read my paper how extremely docile they had been, driving for hours regaled by endless talking on the part of the bandit who sat in the back seat with his gun poised behind their ears. At the time I felt some contempt that all they had been able to do by way of attracting attention was to turn on the reversing light of the car. They had even stopped for petrol! In the end the man had been shot dead and the young woman left for dead and I distinctly remember thinking that I, personally, would never have let it come to that.

Alas! I was lamentably biddable, continually having to keep myself from shouting at them to put the guns away, one of them might go off. Watchful for the moment when I might snatch the gun and reverse the position, yet aware that they too were watchful for such a move on my part. The strong acid of fear running down from my brain and washing over my gastric ulcer was giving me hellish indigestion; one of the least of our troubles.

Juniper was utterly cool, emotionless, immaculate, unbent, uncracked, her behaviour was beyond praise. I

THE DAY OF THE DONKEY DERBY

began to feel I couldn't stand much more of this, I should charge about, hitting wildly, shouting, breaking things, and getting myself shot would be a happy release. I couldn't *wait* any longer; I'm notoriously impatient, I'm not good at waiting for babies to be born, like so many good GPs. I hate hanging around for hours and hours, smiling cheerfully and saying: 'You're doing splendidly, Mrs So-and-So!' I have to do it but it always gives me indigestion. Knowing for certain that the baby is coming doesn't relieve one; as I knew for certain now that the police were coming. It makes it worse, somehow.

I am wondering now if Rainbarrow really meant to go. He'd left home before; recently he had been out to Torremolinos and stayed there a while during the building of Micky's block of flats. But the Spanish servants had been left at home, looking after the lovebirds. This time he had to take the birds with him, in spite of all Micky's protests.

Further, he was suddenly obstinate about going away in the van; he remembered it was unlucky, he said. Even with new trade plates he decided he wouldn't risk going anywhere in it, it was better in the stable, and as far as he was concerned it should stay there. The only way of getting at Nell Fitton's car was for Micky to fetch it. Unless he, Micky, would go on Rainbarrow's tricycle (a ludicrous idea, apparently), there was nothing for it but to walk to the main road and thumb a lift to the village where the car was parked. 'You don't know much about walking, so try running,' he said sarcastically.

So Nell Fitton would have to be let out now because she had the only available key of her car.

'Now don't panic, Mick, don't panic,' Rainbarrow urged, 'there's nothing to worry about. Can't you get it into your head that whatever rumours the police may have about me now, they're not going to come tearing along and search the house now. It's Saturday evening, boy, at the end of the first fine day we've had this year... it would take the sergeant all day to get a search warrant and they can't enter the house of a perfectly respectable citizen until they have one!'

'Look, Uncle – ' Micky bent towards his uncle, very tense, speaking slowly as though to someone half-witted – 'we can't let Nell Fitton out now. There's far too many people hanging about; these two, for instance. We've not been alone more than a couple of minutes since I entered this house, and in that time Doctor Lavenham managed to do quite a bit of damage in the drawing-room. We don't want to add to the crowd!'

'Then how are you proposing to start Nell Fitton's car?'

Then he remembered that Molly would sometimes drive Nell Fitton's car, and leaving us covered by his uncle's Luger he went upstairs to search Molly's handbag. He came down, dejected, and carrying the ticket reservations for the night flight, which he had evidently forgotten. 'No key.'

I was longing for Nell Fitton to be let out, if only for a change of face and there would then be three of us against two. Rainbarrow pulled out a pew-like chair from under the communion table and slumped down on it. 'I'm tired,' he said simply. 'I've been up since six this morning and there's been no let-up. I'm tired!'

'Tell me the safe number,' Micky said slyly, 'and I'll let the girl out then.'

He ignored that but got up and staggered out, as though worn out; indeed he was.

8.50 P.M.

I watched Nell Fitton's entrance through the swing door with interest. As she came in she was, to me, like one risen from the dead. When I had last seen her, so very long ago, she had been so neat, so smart, so reserved, so buttoned-up; her hair smooth and shining, her clothes spotless, her shoulder-bag over her shoulder. The only thing that still obtained was her shoulder-bag over her shoulder. Her clothes were creased and covered with dust, her eye-black smudged all over her cheeks, her face tear-stained, her hair a dusty tangle, her stockings laddered, the toes of her neat shoes scraped and scratched. She looked round at us, smiling wanly at me and saying: 'Dr Lavenham! Still here?'

'This is my future daughter-in-law.' I introduced Juniper proudly, and the two girls eyed one another obliquely. 'She is a doctor, too. And we still haven't been able to come to any decision . . .'

'About what?'

'About anything,' I said, 'and least of all about who killed Molly.'

'I did,' she said simply, 'accidentally!'

'There you go!' Rainbarrow shouted. 'I've finished with you, you stupid girl.'

'I've finished with *you*.' It was a rather stupid *tu quoque* but she had evidently emerged from the silver safe in a different frame of mind from the one in which she had entered it.

'We don't want to know what you did, my girl, we

only want the key of your car. Micky and I are leaving the country for a short holiday, we want to borrow your car to take us to the airport.'

Micky went across to her and there was a trace of the old blarney, the fatal charm about the way he spoke: 'Listen, Nell Fitton, you've ruined me all right. I've shot a policeman and killed him. It's what you've always meant to do, isn't it, ruin me? I can see that now. Well, you've done it this time. But just let me get away. I don't want a lifer, not at my age I don't. And you don't really – *not really* – want me to be punished all that much.' He paused, waiting, and the expression on Nell Fitton's face was like that on the face of Sir Galahad, in that awful picture, as he finds the Holy Grail.

It was pure – no, perhaps pure isn't quite the word – it was admiration.

9.00 P.M.

'Come on, come on!' Rainbarrow fumed, 'come out with that car key, girl. You're asking to be shot . . .'

She turned on him: 'You devil,' she cried. 'You knew that light goes out when you shut the safe door, didn't you? You *knew* it . . . I've been there in the dark all those hours . . .'

'. . . and damn good for you, too . . .'

'It's you who have ruined Micky, it's you, you at the bottom of everything that has happened. It was you who ruined Molly . . .'

'Me!' Rainbarrow was outraged, the Luger flagging in his fingers.

'Look out!' Micky shouted, and Rainbarrow brought the pistol sharply back into position. 'Now, Nell Fitton, keep your head. All you're asked to do is to produce the key of your car. We need it.'

'And leave me here in this house? No fear! You're going to put me back in there again. I'd rather shoot myself . . .' She was undoubtedly more than slightly hysterical. 'Let me go with you, Micky,' she pleaded.

'Where to?'

'To . . . just to get the car; I want to tell you everything, I want to explain what happened.'

'The nerve of it!' They stared at one another for an abnormally long time. 'Come on, then.'

Rainbarrow grunted as he once more covered us two, then shouted over his shoulder: 'Go on then, boy, and get back as quickly as you can. If the police come while you're away, leave them to me. I'm an old friend of theirs; they can't force an entry and they won't want to when I've finished talking to them!'

9.05 P.M.

I looked longingly out of the door as they walked out, the sun had gone more than half way round the house since I came this morning; there was now a large patch of shade across the drive. Rainbarrow slammed the hall door shut and shot the big central bolt with one hand, the other still steadily covering us. It was a heavy pistol and he had been holding it fairly steady for what seemed to me to be the best part of the day; he must have been longing to put it down.

'Go on into the study,' he said wearily; he was showing more distinct signs of fatigue, I was glad to see. We flung ourselves into the easy chairs like travellers; the room was almost unbearably hot and stuffy.

Juniper started talking; she leaned forward in her chair and talked to Rainbarrow in a low monologue. I was listening acutely but I did not manage to hear everything she said, she was so clearly talking to him rather than to me. She was repeating some of the things she had already said about the way of life of an old man who was not in the best of health. She asked him to tell us exactly what had happened about Molly. She said that on the drive back from the station the Spaniard Paco had told her quite a lot in limping English but it was important that they, she and I, should know the truth.

Rainbarrow replied that he didn't see why. Dr Lavenham's presence at the house today had been a mistake; he should never have been called in. It had been a mad idea, a temporary measure, a false move.

'You're tired,' Juniper said, so low that I could hardly hear. 'You need a good sleep. You don't really want to go away with Micky, do you? You're only going to save him from possible arrest, aren't you?' Her voice went on . . . and on . . . and on . . . I began to wonder if I were going off to sleep and I roused myself by wondering if those two, hurrying on foot down the drive and perhaps getting a lift along the main road to where Nell Fitton's car was parked, would meet the police on their way here. And if so, would the police recognize the man they were looking for? No, they wouldn't be looking for two pedestrians, they would be keeping a watch for the hired green van.

Rainbarrow jumped up suddenly and shook himself, as though rousing himself from unwanted drowsiness. He went to the television, across the corner of the room, and turned it on again.

Juniper looked reproachful: 'I was talking to you . . .'

'I know,' Rainbarrow returned uneasily.

I got the message now: she was trying hypnosis on him. A medical journal had published an article on the subject only a few weeks ago, and I remembered. Chinese doctors, it said, used hypnosis continually, it was commonplace in Chinese doctoring.

It was obvious that he had turned on the television as a distraction to Juniper's insistent small voice. But he slumped down in the chair again and stared sulkily across at her. I could only now hear scraps of what she was saying: 'It is such a pity you don't play chess . . . yes, all my family play but my brothers play Fan-tan with their friends . . . sometimes it is so serious, a player will stake his finger . . . I don't know how much my father weighs but he is not a big man like you . . . he is bald, his head is like a polished stone and now he wears European glasses with deep frames . . .'

She had the tiny travelling birdcage still with her, it was on her knees, and as she talked she stared down at the birds, touching it occasionally with the tips of her long, pointed fingernails.

I had seen a demonstration of hypnosis at a medical lecture and in each case the hypnotist stared the patient straight in the eyes. I made certain that Juniper could not possibly be successful because she did not look directly at her subject all the time. But she kept on talking.

The television seemed to me a complete diversion, it clacked and clamoured away in its corner in a programme of the utmost banality, such as one might expect on a fine hot summer Saturday afternoon with sport on both channels.

Not more than, at a guess, one in three people are susceptible to hypnosis and they have to be willing subjects. Rainbarrow was in a state of tension and excitement. If Juniper had looked across at me I should have shaken my head, letting her know that I thought it unlikely that she would succeed.

I tried to reckon how long it would take the two to return in Nell Fitton's car, travelling the route with them in my mind's eye. Half an hour, perhaps? Less if they were lucky enough to get a bus. They should be back fairly soon . . .

'You're tired . . . it is so hot . . . you are sleepy now . . . why not relax . . . That gun you are holding, it is so heavy . . . so heavy . . . you have been holding it for so long . . . why not let your arm rest along the arm of your chair? . . . you must be so tired of holding it . . . it has been a long day . . . please turn off the television . . .'

I realized that the last remark was addressed to me but Rainbarrow was not yet quite oblivious of his surroundings. He barked: 'Don't move!' adding, rather more sleepily: 'Either of you.'

It was our last hope, apart from the arrival of the police, and I had begun to despair that they would ever arrive in time. I noticed that Rainbarrow's hand was resting along the arm of the chair. Given time, I began to think, she might do it, but there isn't time. I crept over to the television and turned it off. There was an insidious rhythm, a treacherousness about the sound of her voice now that was certainly beginning to affect me.

'You're so tired ... you've got a long journey ahead but you're so, so very tired ... give me the gun ... give me the gun ... give me the gun ... you're tired, so very tired ... your eyelids are heavy as lead ...'

Well, if his weren't, mine certainly were. I moved away and sat with my back to them by the window; I did not want to listen to that crafty and subtle whispering: 'Give me the gun ... give me the gun ... give me the gun ...'

'How do you open the silver safe ... how do you open it ... what combination do you use ... tell me ... tell me ...'

I was beyond listening, I was only hearing. I had to hear it three times before I did anything about it; her voice did not alter by one semitone. 'What combination of figures or letters do you use, take-the-gun-father-in-law ... take-the-gun-father-in-law ... take-the-gun-father-in-law ...'

I felt a great useless clumsy oaf, I could hear my bones crack as I stood up with the minimum of movement, moved across the room, slid the gun from his now nerveless fingers.

One gets light trances, medium trances and deep trances and she was now testing the degree with one not very sharp prong of the tortoiseshell pin she had taken from her hair. Now I actually had the Luger in my hands I examined it carefully; I am not at all at home with pistols.

She was still uncertain what degree of unconsciousness she had achieved in her subject because, though she nodded to me, she did not stop talking softly: 'You're tired . . . just rest awhile, keep your eyes closed, your lids are so heavy, so heavy, so heavy . . . tell me the combination that opens your safe . . .' She had got him all right, his head was stiff in a cataleptic condition rather than that of one dozing.

A patient of mine who had been suffering from hysterical amnesia had been completely cured by a hypnotist to whom I had sent him in London; I was extremely interested in the present neat demonstration but the weight of the damned pistol in my hands reminded me that there were more important things to do.

I got my priorities wrong: I went to the telephone first; they had probably been right when they had sneered at my 'respectability', assuring one another that I would 'die of it'. I nearly did. I'm not making excuses for myself when I say I think a GP has to hold firmly to the umbrella of respectability beneath which he shelters, there are too many opportunities for him to be disreputable. Beneath all the worries I had had during this curious day I think the most important one was the possibility of a criminal charge against me, and I confess that I had to get that dismissed from my mind even before telephoning to relieve my wife's anxieties.

As I stood listening to the ringing note (the Coroner was out, of course, on this lovely holiday evening; probably only lying in a deckchair in his garden, a newspaper over his face to keep off the evening midges) I put down the telephone receiver and with the other hand loosely grasping the gun I went to the front door and shot back the door bolt. Micky came in followed by Nell Fitton. He entered with his gun held in front of him and stared at the scene in amazement.

'Put down what you are holding, Doc,' he commanded briskly, and I, meek as the people I had criticized in the A6 murder, because I didn't know how to use the damn thing anyway, did as he asked. He picked up the Luger from the desk before turning to his uncle.

'What is wrong with him?' He bent down, trying to look into the old man's face. 'Is he ill? Has he had a stroke?' he asked and with mounting anger demanded to know what we had done to him. Juniper stood a little apart, holding the tiny birdcage; she had the air about her of someone modest but mildly proud, as her handiwork was admired.

'Uncle! Uncle!' Micky shook his arm but there was no response.

'Take care!' Juniper said.

'Do you want to kill the old man?' I demanded indignantly. 'He is hypnotized . . . if you try to wake him you'll probably kill him, in his state of health.' Not true, of course, but he was not to know that.

'You Chinese witch!' He turned on Juniper, apparently not in any doubt who was responsible.

'Our secret weapon,' I said smugly, 'our form of sabotage; he obviously can't go with you now, can he?'

'He must . . . he must.' Micky was like a spoiled child, something which I had remarked upon before, but now it was very evident. His behaviour was distinctly non-adult, he was almost crying with frustration. I was not surprised to see an air of quiet triumph about Nell Fitton, towards whom, after a lot of false starts, I was beginning to feel an active dislike. Micky knelt down in front of his uncle and putting both hands on his knees he stared up into his face, willing him to wake up.

'So you were the abortionist,' I said to Nell Fitton, 'a State Registered nurse and probably a certified midwife. I don't think much of your attempt!'

'And I don't think much of you as a doctor!' she flashed back.

'Much better men than I have been mistaken about the time of death. Rigor mortis was beginning to set in round her face only when I last saw the body, that would be a good seven hours after death!'

'Seven hours!'

'Go on,' I urged. It was interesting medically apart from any other consideration.

'I was on night duty last night, I came off duty early and brought the instrument home with me from hospital. She wanted me to do it, she begged me, she was desperate. So I did it, shortly after a rest...' She looked thoughtful, sad.

'Go on!'

'She was convinced she would be all right in a few hours.'

'You told her so?'

'Well, yes... I've known people walk home after it.'

'Never when they are as far gone!'

'She insisted that I do it. She talked long past midnight.'

'Don't try to fool me. You knew perfectly well she wouldn't be well enough to go to Spain tonight.'

'Well, perhaps I did!' she snarled. 'Perhaps I did. She was too stupid to run along with Micky, anyway. She'd told me the whole plan.' The expression on her face was repulsive. 'You've no idea how stupid she was; she didn't think about anything but clothes and make-up and a good time. I was fond of her, very fond of her, but . . .' She tailed off. There was no doubt that she had been deeply shocked by what had occurred.

'You won't be able to avoid a criminal charge, you know,' I reminded her. 'So you had better tell me what happened; it will help you in the end to have told me.'

She wanted to tell me, she turned towards me again soberly. 'Around dawn I gave her 0.5gm Pentothal and within a few seconds of my starting the operation she . . . well, I couldn't believe it . . . she stopped breathing.'

I nodded.

'She stopped breathing!' she wailed.

'Functional,' I said. 'You weren't really to blame, you shouldn't have attempted it in the first place.'

'If you only knew, if you only knew . . . what I went through!'

'So what did you do next?'

'Later, when it was dark, I carried her down to my car, which was outside in the mews beside our front door. She's no weight at all. I brought her case too, all ready packed as it was. I couldn't leave here there, I'd telephoned yesterday to her mother in Ireland to come and look after her and I knew she'd come. So there was no alternative but to bring her here, I could not let the anxious mother find the girl dead! I laid her on the back seat and covered her with a rug to keep the body temperature up, it was such a hot night. I've been here once before, we both came down one day for lunch with Micky and his uncle. I thought he'd be able to help me. I got here fairly early this morning, somewhere between six and a quarter-past, and fortunately the old man was up and about. He opened the door to me and together we carried Molly upstairs. He had to help me, there was no way out of it. It was he who thought of you, he said we'd pass the buck. It only took me an hour and a half to get here, at that time of day. He arranged the room, the pyjama trousers and all that, he unpacked the case and left it looking as though she'd arrived last night. Then he told me to go into the village and get myself a cup of coffee at the local and leave my car there and come back later pretending I'd come by train. The Spaniards were around by the time I left and I knew they were surprised. I wonder just how much they guessed.'

'You're a wicked girl really,' I observed thoughtfully, 'because you'd have been quite content to let the blame rest on, as it happened, me.'

'It's every woman for herself in this rat-race,' she said bitterly. 'I want my place in the sun, just like any other girl, and time's going on . . . I'm twenty-seven and I've done nothing all my life but slog and slog away at nursing.'

'Some people love it.'

'They're the dedicated ones. I don't like being bossed around, I want to be the boss just sometimes and there's no chance of it where I am; the sisters have it all their own way!'

'So you're all set for your "place in the sun"?'

'Molly has had nothing but that ever since she grew up. I didn't think there was much harm in ridding her of a baby which was what she so badly wanted me to do and leaving her in bed getting over it while *I* helped Micky to get his loot through the customs . . . for a change.'

'Oh God,' I groaned, 'perhaps after all I'm glad I never had a daughter.'

It had taken a lot longer to write this scrap of conversation with Nell than it actually took, which was not more than a minute. I was fascinated by what she told me but at the same time aware that during the time Micky was on his knees, staring anxiously into the old man's face, Juniper slipped from the room, now darkening and shadowy. When Nell finished talking and went across to lean down over the old man as well, Juniper was back.

'Come,' I said, 'we must be on our way. Do you feel like walking down the drive in those absurd shoes?'

9.35 P.M.

And then...

What a day it was! I can't say never a dull moment because there were, in fact, a lot of dull moments: waiting, waiting, waiting... can be dull. Waiting for the police to come; or was it waiting for the world outside, basking in the unaccustomed sunshine under a brassy blue sky, to realize that violence was taking place, people were dying in car accidents, getting shot at, robbing, even murdering... and all day I had been impatiently waiting for someone to be doing something about it. We could see the roofs of the trains passing every so often and yet we felt as isolated and out of it as though we were alone in the Sahara with a bunch of cannibals.

It wasn't a question of asking for whom the bell tolled, nobody heard the blessed bell tolling. I turned on the box and put my arm across Juniper's cool, slim shoulders and felt less lonely.

The television was silent for the moment, then a still, prior to the newsreel, was being shown. A voice was asking us if we had seen this man, Micky Flanagan, and there followed his various aliases, whom the police wished to interview with regard to the shooting of a policeman in the East End of London earlier in the day.

It was quite a good photograph taken as he sat at the driving wheel of the hired van, as I learned later.

The first thing, in fact the only thing, I felt immediately was an immense relief that somebody had, in fact, been doing something other than sunbathing this afternoon.

The photograph vibrated, a bluish, leaden colour in front of our stricken eyes for what seemed an immeasurable period of time. Mr Rainbarrow lolled in his chair, mercifully unconscious of his surrounding. The item ended with Scotland Yard's own special amen: 230-1212.

'What are we going to do? What on earth are we going to do?' Micky wailed. The nurse, with the calm efficiency of the theatre probationer, had taken the Luger from him and was moving the safety-catch on, off, on, off. Making sure, not how it worked, but simply that it worked.

I remarked: 'You never wake a hypnotized subject forcibly . . you leave them to sleep it off!'

'Sleep it off . . . but when the police come?'

'Look, Micky, there is nothing we can do but leave him to wake up on his own, unless you'd like to shoot him,' the woman put in sarcastically. 'But, of course, you couldn't do without him, could you?'

'Blast you, bloody woman, blast you!' he wept.

'And now you'll have to have me with you,' she added with quiet triumph and I gathered from the way she said it that during their walk to get the car they had talked it over and he had refused her offer of help.

In a last feeble attempt to delay them a little longer, I reminded him about the track suit. 'Don't forget to take it with you, or, better still, drop it out of the car on your way to the airport. If they search the house . . .'

'Shut your big mouth, will you? Talk, that's the only thing you can do.'

I wondered if he could be right.

'We've got to get rid of these people,' Micky said desperately, 'you can help me over this, Nell Fitton. They've got in my hair long enough; they'll stop our getting away if it's humanly possible . . . or even by witchcraft,' he added, looking at Juniper meaningfully.

He went over to the nurse. 'You're not going to turn soft, are you?'

I thought, this is going to be like the end of Romeo and Juliet with the dead falling upon the dead, as though Shakespeare, suddenly sick of the chattering lot, cleared the stage of his characters by killing them off and gave them a final contemptuous nudge with the shocking bit of sub-nursery-rhyme verse:

> *For never was a story more of woe*
> *Than this of Juliet and her Romeo.*

9.45 P.M.

The sun had gone, it was blackbird time; through the closed window I could hear its requiem.

'Things are bad enough, Micky, why make them worse,' she said, 'by killing them?'

'What else can we do?'

'The silver safe . . .'

'Did my uncle shut the door when he let you out?'

She looked blank.

'I can't remember . . .'

'If he did, I can't open it. He's never trusted me with the combination, nor anyone else, for that matter.'

Like the slow paces to the gallows we walked together, Juniper and I, ahead of them, with the guns pointing at our backs. Absurdly the first words of the burial service started to run through my head: *Man that is born of woman . . . he fleeth as it were a shadow and never continueth in one stay.* I had heard them so often and never noticed how bewitching they were. I had my arm across Juniper's shoulders and I hoped, knowing that they might not, that the shots might be more or less simultaneous, that neither of us would be the first to drop away from the other.

But as we went through the swing door and into the service corridor we both saw the door of the safe hanging open, the light streaming out.

I don't know what was going on behind my back but I think probably Nell Fitton stopped him from shooting, insisting that we should go into the safe alive.

The electric fan was still going; momentarily I saw the

shelves down either side bearing their lumpy green felt bags with tape draw-strings, and the leather-covered cases of various shapes. I also saw a packing case against the wall at the end. I feel certain that there was acute disagreement between the two behind us, they were probably arguing with gestures. It was a relief when the door slammed behind us and we were in darkness.

Sheer built-in decorum caused me to take my arm away from Juniper's shoulders. I stared hard at where I thought she was, in the darkness.

'Well, that's it,' I said cheerfully, 'and it isn't quite sound-proof, you heard Nell Fitton shouting this afternoon, didn't you?'

'Faintly, yes...'

I groped my way to the packing case. 'Come and sit down on this box, I don't know about you but my knees are feeling distinctly weak.'

We sat, recovering, in silence for a long time. I think I said something like: 'When you're sure you are going to die and you're still hale and hearty, life suddenly seems full of magic and enchantment that you've missed, even the burial service.'

But I was thinking: how will we ever get out? When the old man wakes up he will never hear our shouts. Perhaps it would have been better if we had been shot.

I pondered, too, upon the miracle of finding the safe door open; how could he have left his precious safe open even for a few minutes? I'm still wondering about it...

'Now you are not to worry too much, there is something I will tell you: the criminal Micky and that woman who calls herself a nurse thought only of themselves. They observed nothing, they only wished what each one wished.' And in the dark she gently took my hand.

'Only *you* observed that I left the room and in a few minutes I returned. During that time no gun was pointing at me, I was free. But nobody saw me take the shabby card from the old man's breast pocket before I left the room.'

'The card!' I snarled, or almost, feeling hopelessly inadequate.

'A shabby card, or would you say a grubby card? And guess what? It was the card upon which he had at some time written the number to open the safe door. It was nonsense to hear Micky say that no one knew the number of the door. Maybe several people know. I know, it's here.'

She led my hand to the edge of the card she held. 'Can you feel it? He kept it in the breast pocket of his jacket. I took it as he started to lose consciousness and with the telephone pencil and in those few minutes I left the room I wrote the number in big letters on the back of a used envelope lying on his desk. And I ran into the drawing-room with the smashed window and tucked it tight in the marble hand between finger and thumb of the woman who is also a jewel container to which you drew my attention . . . remember. She was face down among all the broken glass but I stood her up again and anyone – *anyone* – would at once see it. They did not notice even that I left the room, those two . . . It was still daylight but I turned on every electric light switch I passed though it was broad daylight.'

The enormous relief that somebody, just somebody might know that we were rotting in the safe was enough to cause me to fall asleep; since dawn I had been abnormally awake every second of this horrible day. I slept. Juniper sat beside me on the box straining her utmost to translate the sounds she was faintly hearing.

11.35 P.M.

I woke wishing very much I could see my watch. Something had woken me, some sound. Juniper was a light weight against my shoulder, asleep perhaps or perhaps not. I had woken sharply thinking about our Miss Cloverley-ffane with her absurd name. She would be back from her picnic, would have said goodbye to her friend and would be at my home. She would be talking to my wife, to my son. I hoped he was not tearing madly about the countryside in a police car . . . no, I could not visualize what was happening. I saw, in my mind's eye, Clover making pot after pot of tea and mouthing endless inanities, the main subject being 'the dear Doctor'.

My Labrador would be lying on the floor in the hall with a black paw pressed to either side of his floppy mouth; which would denote extreme dissatisfaction with everyone present.

And then I heard a faint sound, as of someone winding a clock. The heavy door swung slowly open outwards, the light went on and the fan, simultaneously. Holding a used envelope with numbers on it and with shaking fingers, stood our Clover, as though by thinking of her I had summoned her from our kitchen.

'Oh, Doctor!' she exclaimed. 'Whatever have you been up to?'

Juniper and I stared at her wordless.

'Mrs Lavenham and Robin are with the police; they've found your car . . . everybody thinks you've been kidnapped . . .' There was a pause until the next bit of arbitrary information. 'There's a bobby in the hall waiting for the telephone to ring; they're expecting someone to ring us about ransom money for you!' With wide-open eyes and less wide-open mouth she stared at us; she was aghast.

There was no need to ask her, I knew what had happened. So often in the past that little woman, curiosity itself, had lifted up a telephone receiver as it rang (one of the four telephones in our house) listened for a moment and replaced it. It had so often annoyed me that once I challenged her with it most disagreeably. But often I greatly regretted having done so because there were occasions when it was extremely important that someone in the house should know 'where the doctor was' or 'who the caller was' or what the call was about. It was just such an occasion early this morning when the doctor answered the telephone and the listening Clover, picking up another phone, registered that his presence was required by that funny old Mr Rainbarrow of Dedend.

'If I hadn't lifted the receiver this morning when the phone rang, you see, Doctor . . . as it was, as soon as I got home this evening, less than an hour ago, I was able to say: "Leave it to me!" '

Leave it to her to drive the seven miles to Dedend at a good pace and at once notice the smashed window, to creep 'on tip-toe' as she called it, through the broken glass in the big room; leave it to her to step over the wreckage and peer at the fallen woman, the stone caryatid, who hid the surplus jewels that our Rainbarrow had not brought himself yet to dispose of. Leave it to her to snatch the shabby card and to dial the number which would open the silver safe in the service corridor.

'But is the old man mad?' Clover asked, rearranging her face. And now she stared fascinated at Robin's girl and I introduced her formally to Clover as my future daughter-in-law: '... who has been here since she arrived at the station from London in the early afternoon. Her presence has no doubt saved my life.'

Since Clover had indulged in this prodigal turning on of lights I felt once again my normal self. Incredibly it was only just past eleven-thirty. I stood at the hall telephone and quite normally rang the hospital to send an ambulance for old Mr Rainbarrow at once. I told them he was lying in an armchair in his study at Dedend; the lights were on but nobody would be in the house. I told them I was unable to wait for the ambulance as I had been here all day but I would come to the hospital first thing in the morning. I said the night ambulance people were to tell Dr Shaw that Mr Rainbarrow was in a hypnotic coma from which he would probably have emerged by morning, when he could be given a cup of tea, no other treatment was necessary before my visit.

I rang my home, a detective answered.

EPILOGUE

A busy GP is not satisfactory kidnapping material, as Robin pointed out to his mother to her great comfort. He also assured his mother that Juniper Ah Mee, apart from her brains and her charm, was a totally reliable person. The two doctors were, therefore, welcomed home with great love and assurance. Clover was in a state of muted ecstasy, pouring out drinks for them all, even a small glass of whisky for herself.

Dr Lavenham gave what amounted to a short speech of praise for his womenfolk and the warmest of thanks. He did not believe that he would have emerged from that strange house, oddly and aptly named Dedend, if it were not for Clover and Juniper. He hoped they would forgive him if he told them now nothing about what had happened between eight-thirty a.m. and half past eleven p.m. in that deadly house; he would like time to think it over. He wanted to take tomorrow off and lie in bed thinking and making notes. He would like his wife to telephone to Dr Shaw in the morning to ask him to take over his patient Rainbarrow because he never wished to see the man again. Dr Lavenham did not think that Rainbarrow could survive for long the life he was leading.

Micky Flanagan was arrested while standing alone at the airport watching a plane take off for Spain. Later he received a stiff sentence and was sent to Parkhurst.

The case of the two Spanish servants: the man driving Dr Lavenham's car at great speed admitted he had never driven in his life. The accident was considered to be a tragedy in which the woman lost her life and the man a leg. Foul play was not suspected.

Dr Lavenham remembered that he had a bribe of five hundred pounds in his notecase. Would somebody please relieve him of it in favour of Guide Dogs for the Blind or any other good cause.

Juniper drew their attention next, she was carrying a small thing from which she whisked the scarf which covered it. The two small birds were shivering and close together. 'I stole this,' she said and asked if she might keep it.

One can say with confidence that Nell Fitton lived happily ever after, not as a nurse but on the treasure she quickly annexed from the marble woman in the drawing-room just before they left and because she replaced the card with the safe numbers on it.

Is there a hero in this tale of woe?

No.

But there is a heroine whom we have only heard of as speaking on the telephone, nor have we heard what she said. It was Lady Lakeland, the mother of Molly, who loved her daughter exceedingly and who, aided by some very good friends, removed her daughter from the house called Dedend early in the morning after the day of the Donkey Derby by hired Daimler, procured a death certificate with the help of a good friend of hers, a gynæcologist in Harley Street, arranged for her body to be flown to her home and buried with love and honour in their Irish village.

And when peace had fallen upon the Lavenham house, one last thought struck open the doctor's eyes: 'Damn, I quite forgot the hurdles for the Donkey Derby.'

'Everybody rushed to do it for you, darling,' his wife chuckled, 'and they will bring them all back today for you, you'll see!'